Leap-seconds

Leap-seconds

Paul Zits

Leap-seconds

Gillian,

Still a little allergic to
this planet. (but
so pleased to know you).

SEROTONIN | WAYSIDE

INSOMNIAC PRESS

Library and Archives Canada Cataloguing in Publication

Zits, Paul, author
Leap-seconds / Paul Zits.

Short stories.
Issued in print and electronic formats.
ISBN 978-1-55483-187-6 (softcover).--ISBN 978-1-55483-201-9
(PDF)

I. Title.

PS8649.I87L43 2017   C813'.6   C2017-904107-X
                                             C2017-904108-8

The publisher gratefully acknowledges the support of the
Canada Council for the Arts and the Ontario Arts Council.

Printed and bound in Canada

Insomniac Press
520 Princess Avenue, London, Ontario, Canada, N6B 2B8
www.insomniacpress.com

THE CANADA COUNCIL | LE CONSEIL DES ARTS
FOR THE ARTS | DU CANADA
SINCE 1957 | DEPUIS 1957

ONTARIO ARTS COUNCIL
CONSEIL DES ARTS DE L'ONTARIO

For my mother

We are in a *flat* and *discontinuous* universe where each thing refers only to itself. A universe of fixity, of repetition, of absolute obviousness, which enchants and discourages the explorer....

— Alain Robbe-Grillet, *For a New Novel*

time? goldenberg said in astonishment, and several days later, after thinking the matter over, he said, it is just a cutting-up of the whole, by means of the senses.

— Konrad Bayer, *the sixth sense*

I prefer Grimms' fairy tales to the newspapers' front pages.

— Wisława Szymborska, "Possibilities"

Fair reader I offer merely an analogy. A delay.

— Anne Carson, *The Beauty of the Husband*

Contents

Part One

Room 227

The end.

—Sergio González Rodríguez, *The Femicide Machine*

•

The place was aglow with red and blue lights, with the naked body arched across the old mattress. Face up and dead, she was naked except for an unlaced pair of worn-out blue-green high-top sneakers. Her body was sprawled sideways across an old mattress from which her head dangled into the bottles & leaves. Red and blue lights upon her while she slumbered. Red and blue lights upon her as if she speaks. Like a gas flame, upon her throat, a four-pointed star. Like a cardinal's robe, upon her head. Like a garland of lupins, upon her arm. Red and blue lights upon her while she slumbered. Like a tomato, upon her breast. Like a marble, upon her shoulder. Like a cockatoo's bared crown, upon her rug of fur and her little eyes. Like the turquoise stone in the belly of the

Thunderbird, upon her limbs. Red and blue lights upon the soil, nearby. Like the lining of a crucible upon her neck. Red and blue lights upon her exposed years. Upon her life. Upon her death. Like cold glass upon her heels. Like the worms on which small fish feed upon her breast. Red and blue lights upon her light freckles and short red hair. Like the flames on a gas range upon her head. Full upon her face, a tangled mass. Like a piece of iron cooling in the air, slashing now, upon her face, her head, her chest, and her abdomen, clear down, even to her hands and feet. Red and blue lights upon her hands, indeed as if sleeping. Like jam upon her knee. Like skin that had been badly bruised upon her lips. Like brick upon the plane of her body. Upon her fragile form. Like the touch paper you light, swooping down upon her and then circling like a great gull in the wind. Like the twenty-lira note upon her finger. Like fingernails upon her shoulders. Upon her open palm. Upon her shoulders. Sweeping down upon her shoulders. Like tinsel caught in the breeze upon her canals. Upon her knees. Like a live coal upon her lips. Like a slab of sky off the assembly line upon her face. Like a depot stove in midwinter in her cradle. Like faded grass upon her loveliness and perfection in that setting. Upon her body. Like arterial blood upon her shores. Red and blue light along her small tin pail, nearby. Along her large tin pail, nearby. Like the beryls in the clasp of the Queen's missal along her sides. Like Japanese lacquer along her back. Red and blue lights along her notebook, nearby. Like kingfisher feathers along her side. Along her towering side. Like rubies along her sides. Along her entire body. Like the Sycorax's eyes along her sides. Like a turkey cock along her jawline. Like a ribbon along her side. Like raspberries along her spine. Like the shadow of a woman's eyes along her spine. Like the hands of a woman scrubbing along her throat. Like delphiniums and bachelor's buttons along her spine. Like flashing lightning along her jawline and hooked under her ears. Like radishes along her upper gums. Like the colour given off by burning chemicals along her stomach. Like a cock's comb along her cheekbones. Like neon woven into cloth along her jawline. Like a girl's nipples in love along her freckles. Like roads along her neck. Like crayfish along her upper teeth. Like a sulfur flame along her sides. Like cinnabar along her forearm. Like chalk along her leg. Red and blue lights along her jacket, nearby. Like sundae cherries along her shoulder. Like skimmed milk along her sides. Like the Little Red Spot of Jupiter along her neck. Like the sky after a storm along her shoulder and side. Along her side. Like cobalt glass along her sides. Like a crab along her supine frame. Along her spine. Along her spine. Along her spine. Like rotten meat along her cheeks. Along her cheekbones. Like embers along her temple. Like the back wall of a rat's cage along her waist. Along her waist. Like smoke from a burning building along her body. Like a peacock's neck along her spine. Like the blood of a slaughtered ox along her length. Like a bruise along her eyes, opened then closed. Like some crafty old monkey along her back. Like faded denim along her arm, leg, belly. Like wattles against her abdomen. Like a fig against her head. Like the dawning stain from the East against her bare skin. Like young wheat against her ribs. Like a wound against her cheek. Like dark byssus against her chest. Like pomegranate seeds against her body. Like rippling silk against her shoulder. Like a buffalo skull against her face. Like shadowed waters against her throat. Like surgery against her mouth. Like the inside of a saxophone against her wrist. Like a sausage against her ear. Like a wagon track against her side. Like the stripes in the U.S. flag against her throat. Against her throat. Like a bit of old Delft against her thighs. Like ledger lines against her caved-in chest. Like stars made of thread on a pillowcase against her breastbone. Red and blue lights against her earrings. Like a cactus blossom against her face. Like a fine pale porcelain against her bare belly. Like coral against her skull. Like the shadow of Glaucus against her breast. Like a scalped head against her long, long legs.

Room 227

•

I am in one of the innumerable rooms, and the out-
standing characteristic of these rooms is that the
doors are always open, or nearly always. From this
I recall that at one time, work was done by collabo-
ration, by exchange of ideas. Someone was once as
likely to be working here at six in the morning as at
midnight, if the spirit so moved him, and then possibly he would not appear for several days, when the
spirit moved him elsewhere. At times there would
have been feverish physical activity, with experimental testees following schedules from one room to another as if they were trotting in a maze, calculating
machines ticking away upstairs, and hidden cameras
and microphones recording responses. However the
spirit moves, the doors are always open, or nearly

always. The doors are always open, or nearly always, however the spirit moves. With calculating machines ticking away upstairs, and hidden cameras and microphones recording responses, experimental testees following schedules from one room to another as if they were trotting in a maze, at times there would have been feverish physical activity. When the spirit moved them elsewhere, then possibly they would not appear for several days elsewhere. If the spirit so moved them elsewhere, they were once as likely to be working elsewhere at six in the morning as at midnight elsewhere. The spirit no longer moves them, or moves them about in places further than can be observed. The spirit no longer moves them, or no longer moves them about in places further than can be observed. The spirit moves the feverish physical activity in the calculating machines, the spirit moves the ticking away upstairs, the spirit moves in the cameras and in the microphones recording, in rooms where the doors are always open, or nearly always. Nearly always, the spirit moves. At one time, I am in one of the innumerable rooms. I am in one of the innumerable rooms, at one time.

•

Voice lifts from the recording. The recording is a rubbing. The voicewheel rubbing against the lid. His
voice is tiny compass needles. He hears response in
a recording beneath a recording of non-response.
Yesterday's non-response. The decade's non-response. Ribbons of calculating machines ticking
away upstairs. He hears yesterday's faucet. Tiny
compass needles in the pipes. His hands are fists beneath his pillow. His feet are fists beneath the sheet.
The story faucets from the machine.

●

The stirring of the slatted metal blinds. A breeze unsteadies the bottom rail. A cadence clatters identical with that playing back through the speakers. Greater breezes asphyxiate on the slats. Identical with the playback. The calculating machines ticking away upstairs. Identical. Breezes and greater breezes enter through a gap between the lower sash and the sill. The valance, yellowed and damp, lies at the base of the wall, beneath the window. The window is an interior casing, a head jamb, a side jamb, an upper sash, a sash lock, a lower sash, a top rail, a bottom rail, a stile, a muntin, an exterior sill, a stool, an apron, and panes. The window is six panes in the upper sash and six panes in the lower. Sliding the blinds to the side, exposing the bottom left-hand pane, notice a square of sulfured newsprint pasted to fit precisely within its frame. The fitting of the newsprint has clipped the image of a Zeppelin in half. The engines, rudder, and elevator flap with a blue sky the backdrop. The sun has washed the page of its material. It is pale. The ink is deserting the page. The image is unknotted, nearly vapour. Transparent in the light, muddied with lettering from the backside. The Zeppelin is the bottom left pane of the lower sash. The picture of a painting of Wernher von Braun's wheel-shaped space station design is the bottom middle pane of the lower sash. A pudgy Shakur, "thug life" tattooed across his belly, is the bottom right pane of the lower sash. An image of a painting of a pipe is the top right pane of the lower sash. A reproduction of a painting of Aphrodite, flanked by slave boys, each made to resemble Eros, who cool her with their fans, is the top middle pane of the lower sash. Zindapir, royally clad in blue and crimson Mughal dress, a green turban on his head, riding along the Indus on a palla fish, is the top left pane of the lower sash. The upper sash is revealed by pulling the cord tassel. Lenin is the bottom left pane of the upper sash, seated at the Café de la Rotonde on a cane chair; he has paid twenty centimes for his coffee, with a tip of one sou. He is drinking out of a small white porcelain cup. He is wearing a bowler hat and a smooth white collar.... He is teaching himself to govern one hundred million people. A photograph of a painting of the Last Supper on a grain of rice is the bottom middle pane of the upper sash. Saturn devouring his sons is the bottom right pane of the upper sash. Adolph

Hitler is the top right pane of the upper sash. A reproduction of a painting of dead fish and oysters on a kitchen slab, dominated by the rearing, arched shape of a gutted snake, is the top middle pane of the upper sash. A scenery with a small house in the top left corner is the top right pane of the upper sash. Light comes in, in its pieces, its colours with threads, through the reclining nude, through the arousal, the panicking, the succession of landscapes, the palpable lifelikeness, the skies, the heat and thirst, the ugly blue and orange of the optimum fire. At the doorway looking back, through a door that is always open, or nearly always, a Coninxloo-like scenery, or the sky of a planetarium, washes over the room, the stirring of the slatted metal blinds.

I am allergic to this planet.

— Jean-Pierre Duprey

•

I hear the sound of someone urinating on another floor. It is likely a man because I can hear it so well. But the furnace is running, so I cannot be sure. But a plane is passing overhead, so I cannot be sure. But the insect chatter in the speakers carom, their winged chatter stirring, their abdomens dragging along the surfaces, so I cannot be sure. But I hear the sound of a symphony, of traffic on playback in another room, the sound of paper crinkling, so I cannot be sure. But I hear the sound of breath, of someone softly closing the door of the human voice, so I cannot be sure. But I hear the sound of the bed giving, the sound of the driver's forehead pressed against the windscreen, of an oboe, so I cannot be sure. But I hear the sound of the door closing, the key turning in the lock, the sound of socked feet, so I cannot be sure. But I hear the sound of the faucet again, the sound of the owl, the sound of a dog barking in the distance, so I cannot be sure. But I hear the sound of my own voice, the sound of a car engine, a car door slamming, the sound of a roaring lion, so I cannot be sure. But I hear the sound of an engine, the sound of shoes on the grit, the sounds of insects and clashing pans, so I cannot be sure. But I hear the sound of wood cracking, the sound of a clattering pot as the sound of a clattering pot, of the latch being nailed to the door, so I cannot be sure. But I hear the sound of small arms fire and an interchange with a machine gun, the shower running, the sound of water running off the roof, so I cannot be sure. But I hear the sound of water shooting into a watering can, of boxes being opened, the sound of wooden bats striking horsehide, so I cannot be sure. But I hear the sound of spray curling and leaping as the wave rises to the shore, metal hitting flesh, the sound of birds, of someone cutting a tree, so I cannot be sure. But I can hear a train, the sound of the rolling stool, the sound of the electric motor again as the tip of the huge dildo moves back and forth, the sound of a car, so I cannot be sure. But I hear the sound of an opening door, the sound of the harp and the violin, the sound of urine hitting a bush, so I cannot be sure. But I hear the sound of boots in the hallway, the sound of something that I have never heard before, the sound of two men talking, the sound of friction made by two hands being quickly rubbed together, so I cannot be sure. But I hear the sound of marching soldiers, a dog howling, the sound of gunfire, of the leaves, of fists, of rainwater dripping down from a fissure in the roof, so I cannot be sure. I hear the sound of a trolley, of a fly zipper getting tugged open, of keys jingling, so I cannot be sure. But I hear the sound of a helicopter, of muffled voices, of workmen approaching, so I cannot be sure. But I hear the sound of an operetta dancing in the throat of a slot machine paying off, of a hummingbird's wings, so I cannot be sure. But I hear the sound of bullets ripping through the basket of a hot-air balloon, of rumbling mufflers, of knuckles, so I cannot be sure. But I hear the sound of firing, of the cannon, the sounds of children from behind me, so I cannot be sure. But I hear the sound of horses' hooves on the planks of a wooden drawbridge, of vials and baggies on the floor, of skin slipping, so I cannot be sure. But I hear the sound of a desk drawer opening, an ambulance coming, of tearing pages, so I cannot be sure. But I hear the sound of a sliding door, an orchestra, the sound of typing, the sound of a chair moving, so I cannot be sure. But I can hear the sound of calculating machines ticking away upstairs, the sound of the cameras recording, the sound of microphones recording, the sound of a blackbird, somewhere.

3.1i v/o   A pipe man that
lives in the house.   He's taking his clothes off. Because
he has no clothes.
He threw all his clothes away.
He didn't want no clothes (singsong).   No pants, no
socks, no shoes.   He wants to have a lot of hair
around him.
        He's sitting in a dirty chair with no clothes on.
6 v/o   The mouses are
playing doctor and house.   They are having fun. They have
a doll carriage   They're playing lady and man.
They have a pretty home.   They are eating.
They are playing.   They are pretty.
They   have   coffee   pots   and   spoons   and   plates.
They have clothes. They have two blocks and one ball.   They
have   big ears and pretty chairs.   They are nice mouses.
6.1 v/o   They went up the slide, and the last one doesn't think
the one on top   is going fast enough   so when they get
down   the next time, she is the first one
up the slide.   Then she goes down the slide and she can't get
off,   so the others start to come down.   and
they try to push her off.   And then they finally get her off,
and they get up again and go down,
and the first gets stuck again.   And they try to push,
and when the last one comes down,
the first one goes off. And then the first one goes up again,
and they go down and they go back up.
They can't go down the slide   because one gets stuck
in the middle,   and one goes at the bottom   and tries to push
him up and then goes in the back
and tries to push him down. And then they finally get him off   and
then they go around and play a little   and then they try to
go up the slide   and then go down the stairs. Because there prob-
ebly was a little paste on the slide.
6.6 v/o   Three little monkeys were reading very good.
Suddenly a fourth one came in.
It said, "Oh, they are reading.   What dopes they
are. They never knew   how to fight teachers."
The teacher said,   "You must not disturb them."
They fought
and fought with the teacher, and she said,
"You must go to the cellar and be drowned."
They cried and cried.   The three little monkeys
had finished their books.   She said, "You bad, bad
children.   You must come to be drowned." So she
drowned them
(the bad ones).   The good monkeys finished another
book   in a minute.   Another and another,   seconds
and minutes,   halves of seconds,
fourths of seconds.
Finally they read all the books in the world.
and she said,   "What wonderful children you are."
7 v/o   Once upon a time there
was a mother   and father and little bear
-- Jim, Fuzzy, and Andrea (mother's name).   They
lived happily, but one day   a mean hunter came
along.   Fortunately   there was a big wise
elephant   They all liked him   and he liked them.
He snatched the gun   out of the hunter's hand.
"You aren't going to be any more trouble to animals, so I'm going to put
you   in a real strong jail with big double
bars."   The animals learned how to make guns.
After they made guns, they caught all hunters   that came into the jungle.
After that   people made pots of elephants   and
were nice to them   and fed them in winter
                                    and didn't hurt them   They
lived happily ever after.   A mean man came
in and tried to kill nice people,
but all the elephants came up and grabbed the guns
and hid them four miles down into the ground.
They dug for one year
and hid everything they had in tunnels in the rock.
7.9 v/o   Something wrong with this picture -- the
lion's not wearing the crown.
Once there was a lion who was waiting for a train.
He was very nice-looking.   and he smoked a pipe
and he had a cane.   and he waited.
but the train didn't come.   All of a sudden he heard
the train,   and it was on the other side, so he sat down
again   and he waited and he sat there all
day 'cause the train track was broken and the train   didn't
go through.   He said, "I'm getting
tired,"   and he got up and found out in the
newspaper   that the train track was broken,
and so he went down into his house   and took a long snooze
on the chair like he is doing here   and then he had his supper
and had to wait for his train   till the next day.
Darn old train.   I'll make a moral for it: You can't tell if
it's coming if you don't read.

7.9 y/o   The name of this story is "The Monkey and the
Lion."   One day the monkey was climbing
up on the tree and he saw a lion   — I forgot, it was a tiger —
for a moment, and the lion   — the tiger
is next to the king of beasts   "I want to show the lion that I
could be next to the king of the beasts too.
I'll fight the lion and win."   (Monkey says this).   So
the monkey sharpened up his nails
with a pencil sharpener   and tried to scratch the lion
on the neck to kill him,   but the lion jumped up and pushed him
over,   and lion got the monkey by the tail, rather, the
tiger,   and the monkey had his tail shortened.
And the moral is: If you want to keep your
tail long,
you don't want to fool around with the lion.
7.11 y/o   Once upon a time there
were three little chickens.   All of a sudden they saw a
ghost rooster.   All got scared. The ghost rooster
said,   "I want to eat you," and they all threw their
mush in his face, and the rooster threw the bowls back at them,
and they ran and called the papa rooster.   And the ghost
said, "I'd like to eat you."   "Gobble, gobble, gobble,"
said the turkey.   "I'll eat you, ghost rooster," and he
chopped off his head. And the ghost turned into a man, and he turned on
the chickens
and said, "Ah, nice chickens to eat,"   and they chopped off
the man's head.   and he turned into a chicken
and ate the mush until it was all gone,   and mush went into his
stomach   and came out through his eyes,
and he ate more mush and more mush from the bowl,   but the
bowl was magic and mush bowl kept giving more mush.
Suddenly it gave sugar and more sugar,   then fruit and
fruit and fruit,   and he ate it all and ate
and ate and ate.
And suddenly his stomach popped and he changed into a prince.
7.11 y/o   Once there was a tiger and
he ate everything in sight.   — lucky his paws   were not
in sight.   Tarzan ran into the tree   and a
cheetah ran behind him.   Tarzan jumped on him and the tiger
said,   "Try to kill me." Tarzan said,
                    "I will. Don't eat everything in sight." The tiger
ran to eat a tree one day   and the tree fell and honey ran out.
And the bees swooped into his mouth
and into his stomach   and the tiger tried to roar, but all
he could say was a buzzing sound
from the bees.   He got Tarzan to open his stomach,   but
the lion fell dead.   Tarzan saw him alive again and he said,
"I'll never eat a person again, only honey."   But he had
not learned his lesson from the bees. So he reached for honey and the bee
said,   "I'll sting."
The tiger screamed and fell back and the monkey tickled him in the stomach.
The bees took the honey back,   but the tiger growled
and the bees came down   but ran back because
they did not like to be   in the tiger's stomach.
Then the queen bee said,   "I'll show him my beauty."
She came down, but the tiger ate her.   Then the whole
squad swarmed into his mouth
and he chewed them.   Then a big hornet came in and
stung him on the tongue, but his fangs chewed him.
But one day   the tiger ate poison ivy and died.
7.11 y/o   There was a little baby
and father and mother   and a crib with one baby.
                    Every night they sat down   and
said a prayer.   "How we wish we had two babies."
And said maybe at Christmas,
maybe, we'll get a baby.   One night   they
looked in and saw two babies.   "Oh, it must be a magic cradle.   Oh, no.
Make another wish for a flounder."   The husband caught a
giant flounder   and opened him
and ate him.   "Here's another giant flounder   —
maybe the babies would like to eat it all themselves."
The babies' stomachs almost burst   — stomachs growled.
Stomachs got so high,   couldn't get the cover over them. "Oh,
I don't know what I should do."
The stomachs weighed over fifty pounds,
then bang! There was lots of noise   and the first baby's
stomach   burst open   and the mother and father fell in and said,
"What is this, a firecracker?"
Other baby's stomach went up
and stomach opened and it died.
Maybe if we eat flounder and ate and ate and ate
and ate   — then they fell flat and everything goes
BOOM
and everything splits.   — even the Earth split.

Noema, or Room 227's mural

•

He drew his hands from his pocket.
He drew a line in the middle and painted it yellow.
He drew a round hole and painted it so that it appeared as a pinto with red ears.
He drew a second line and painted it the colour of soil.
He drew a roof on four supports and gave it struts to keep the roof on.
He drew a saw seen more fully from the side and painted it black.
He drew a red arrow and painted it the colour of a blue object.
He drew a blue arrow and painted it red.
He drew a green blotch and painted it over and over again.

He drew a brown blotch and painted it the colour of carpet.

He drew a line inside a man's arm and painted it the colour of cloud formations.

He drew a coin from his pocket the colour of a lilac leaf.

He drew a bunch of lettuce with curly leaves and painted it the colour of the shortwave end of the spectrum with entire absence of colour.

He drew a round head of lettuce and painted it the colour of skin.

He drew a sweet pea vine on a pole and painted it the colour of fire.

He drew a picture of a snake emerging from a toilet and painted it in oils, with a border all around it, and bunches of roses and other flowers over the centre.

He drew a dog and some other animals and painted them gunmetal.

He drew a box and painted it the colour of the light which falls upon it.

He drew a portrait of Lorenzo de' Medici and painted it and put pictures of babies and animals all over it.

He drew a circle on the ground and imagined placing his mother there.

He drew a series of fluttering waves and painted it the colour of cotton.

He drew a line and painted it with a luxuriant beauty and a deep understanding.

He drew a jagged coastline and painted it in festive and bright colours.

He drew a shape he described as a "big fish" and printed his first name.

He drew a train with a little boy in it going to Liverpool and painted it up like a zebra.

He drew a clown and painted it as it ought to be and made it with its head hanging down as if it were eating.

He drew a vessel of fifty thousand medimni burden and painted it the colour of milk.

He drew a circle and painted it the colour of royalty and of the vibrant blood of the living.

He drew a picture of a house where children and a mother lived. "The father died," he said, "just like my house, only my mother died."

He drew a large circle and then, abruptly, put the crayon down, picked up a yellow one, with it drew another circle, smaller and above the first. Then he forsook the yellow crayon for the orange one and used it to make a face — round eyes, a thin line for a nose, another thin line for the mouth, two small half-circles for the ears. He put the orange crayon down, then decided to be more emphatic: He placed it in a box. Resuming with the yellow crayon, he imposed identical features on the upper circle he had earlier made. The yellow crayon, too, was then dispatched to its place of enclosure. Now Bellocq picked up the black crayon, held it for a few seconds poised over the paper, directed it toward and then away from the wall, and after two more such movements, back and forth, laid the crayon to rest on the desk but still held between three of his right hand's fingers. Those fingers moved a bit on the crayon, ready to go, but the mind that makes decisions had not figured out what to do.

He drew a revolver and painted it the colour of informational readout displays.

He drew a savage caricature the colour of Los Angeles.

He drew a hunting knife and painted it peacock blue.

He drew a crowd and painted it the colour of the eyes of an Appaloosa horse.

He drew a triangle enclosing a square and looked at the angles.

He drew a fat wad of crumpled fifty-shekel notes and painted it the colour of the brains of Negroes.

He drew a circuit diagram with a power source, a switch, and two bulbs in series, then completed it by connecting the bulbs to the switch.

He drew a modest but distinctive tower to the right of the doorway the colour of glass.

He drew a breath and painted it the colour of varnish.

He drew a pistol and painted it the colour of occultism.

He drew a T-cross with a man's head on it and painted it red, black, and white.

He drew a small telescope and painted it the colour of light passing through it.

He drew a breath from deep within his lungs and painted it the colour of chalk dust.

He drew a bowie knife and painted it the colour of its surroundings.

He drew a triangle, saying, with no prompting, "This is the whole society."

He drew a woman's face and painted it yellow.

He drew a knife and painted it yellow.

He drew a line and painted it yellow.

He drew a veil of forgetfulness and painted it the colour of distant hills.

He drew a funny little man who was scratching his ear and painted it over and stood back and narrowed his blue eyes and tilted his head and stared hard.

He drew a breath and painted it the colour of beets.

He drew a chair and painted it yellow.

He drew a lash of the whip and painted it so large that it filled the whole room.

He drew a deep and thankful breath and painted it like stone.

He drew a comb and painted it the colour of the supernatural.

He drew a key and painted it the colour of an object seen through a dark tube.

He drew a circle and painted it the colour of paradise.

He drew a crowd and painted it the colour of a pyramid.

He drew a tiny picture of a wolf hiding in a cave. He glued his own fallen hair to the wolf to give it fur.

He drew a small chain of beadlike structures and painted them with the wet yellow paint.

He drew a picture of Mary with her head down the lavatory.

He drew a honeydew melon and a red-fleshed watermelon.

He drew a silver quarter from his pocket and painted it yellow.

He drew a chair and painted it orange.

He drew a nice deep breath and painted it the colour of roasted coffee.

He drew a book and painted it the colour of canned

tuna.

He drew a line in the dust.

He drew a ring around the entire bed to keep off spirits and one around each leg to prove to himself the bed was untouched.

He drew a deep breath and painted it the colour of white wine.

He drew a breath of relief and painted it with many beautiful colours and filled it with living creatures.

He drew a large black tomcat and painted it the colour of the faint end of giant elliptical galaxies.

He drew a circle and painted it in dark, smoky colours.

He drew a series of looping ascending lines that looked vaguely like telephone wires marching up a mountain.

He drew a diagonal line from left to right and painted it as no one had ever painted it before.

He drew a bullet and painted it with DRYLOK paint that was supposed to hold back water.

He drew a rude figure and painted it the colour of life on Earth.

He drew a long breath and painted it white at one end and black at the other and then graded in stripes from both ends until it reached a gray tone in the middle.

He drew a line with his toe.

He drew a cross out of stilettos.

He drew a funny picture of himself with a big fat stomach, and under it he wrote, "Me when I get home and eat Mom's cooking."

He drew a perpendicular line between his words, letting it suffice for a comma or period.

He drew a bottle of rye whiskey and painted it the colour of a hard electron.

He drew a deep, steadying breath and painted it the colour of the ocean as seen from space.

He drew a deep breath the colour of a pixel.

He drew a great breath of relief and painted it the colour of protest.

He drew a breath and painted it the colour of the blue lotus.

He drew a chair and painted it from memory.

He drew a catching breath and painted it white with outlines of black.

He drew a deep breath and painted it brown.

He drew a deep breath and painted it black.

He drew a very deep breath and painted it red.

He drew a picture of the scene and put it in his shirt pocket.

He drew a circle on an earlier drawn face and painted it the colour of nitrate.

He drew a circle, and immediately another one.

He drew a long, ragged breath and painted it a dark jungle green.

He drew a line of blue paint down the middle.

He drew a quick breath and painted it red.

He drew a deep breath and painted it silver.

He drew a shaky line and painted it in bright colours that made it look very new and upscale.

He drew a dozen crossbowmen from some castle and painted them a nice light yellow.

He drew a circle in the air.

He drew a long breath and painted it a light khaki colour with a dark red trim.

He drew a finger going down a woman's spine.

He drew a colourful picture.

He drew a picture that "had all its recognizable parts."

He drew a large-scale plan of the area in which he lived.

He drew a couple of weak breaths and painted them in different colours.

He drew a deep and happy breath of memory, a free breath, and painted it all in one day.

●

The washroom was separated from the attached cell by a raised curb. The water did not pollute the living area. He stepped out from the washroom and listened. Calculating machines ticking away upstairs, and hidden cameras and microphones recording. He took a cigarette from a pack of Pall Malls on the bedside table. He stepped out into the hallway. Curled up in the dim corner of a bench in the hallway, a person-shaped shadow of a woman showed only its profile. He stepped out into the hall. The scraping he heard out in the hallway was even more compelling. He presumed there were birds out in the hallway, pecking at the faded yellow-flowered wallpaper. He listened attentively. He stepped out into the hall for a smoke. He stepped out into the hall, head down. He walked slowly with his head down. He stepped out into the hallway, cast a glance up and down its length. He didn't hear the birds any longer, nor did he see them. Tiny footprints of baby Krsna were drawn with white or coloured powder all along the hallway. A second look showed that the footprints were actually stickers, placed there by child patients. All along the corridor he saw nothing but burning sofas and leather chairs. A second look showed that the fires were actually orange pylons. He stepped out into the dimly lit corridor and, without looking back, closed the door behind him. There was a line of plastic or wooden moulding which ran along the walls of the corridor. Above this moulding, there were several small light-coloured patches of paint or plaster about 20 cm apart. He seemed to come to himself once more when he stepped out into the hall again, closing the door. Photos hung in rows along the walls of the hallway, usually black and whites (a black and white photo of artillery shells stored above ground in a wooded area positioned behind a colour photo of a different wooded area with no weapons; a black and white photo of an unsmiling Jackson Pollock standing next to one of his paintings and looking slightly off to the right, the near side of Pollock's face illuminated by a hard light, and the far side hidden by the long shadow he cast against the canvas; a black and white photo of a badly wrecked car; a black and white photo of a waterfall frozen by the shutter in a smooth rush of white; a black and white photo of a recumbent San Francisco Xavier; a black and white photo of a pop fan; a black and white photo of octopuses hung up to dry on a pole at Thasos on the Aegean Sea; a black and white photo of a bobwhite quail; a black and white photo of Elvis and his father, Vernon, in their first swimming pool; a black and white photo of an empty, rumpled bed). He stepped out into the corridor. The corridor was spanned overhead by a series of muted light bulbs in steel cages. He stepped out into the dark of the hallway in his socks, and the moisture in his socks turned into steam and sensitized his skin. He stepped out into the light of the hall and began methodically getting into the overcoat which he would wear tonight. His overcoat was turned up and covered him to the ears. The light in the corridor had been switched on earlier. He stepped out into the passage. A naked bulb burned in the passageway. He stepped out into the passageway, ducking his head to clear the low lintel, but only moved a pace or two into the gloom before stopping and cocking his head back to listen. Above the lintel was a tree of life, with an empty throne and table awaiting the messiah at its foot. He could hear everything that was being said in the recordings in the unknown apartment above, gramophone music from inside (the horn talking, music from a piano speaking to another, the quick sucking in of breath); he could hear when he shut the door (but had no idea when); he could hear a faint nagging hum as of telegraph wires in the wind (the sound in his head, the muscles along the front of his thighs); he could hear certain sounds slightly, every movement ever made in that room; he could hear the full moon (and imagined an ocean pounding against pilings); he could hear the sound of water rushing over the raised curb and felt his feet getting wet; he could hear a rattler, its crisp rustling coming only from inside Room 227; he could hear the dogs panting out in the yard (although it had been years since the yard had dogs); he could hear Czech through an open window, but all the windows were closed; he could hear the unsteady chugging of a motor (chooga-choog, chooga-choog noises) coming from inside Room 225; he could hear a faint sound of chanting, pounding wildly above the din of the motor; he could hear as if he, too, were in the room; he could hear Room 127's booming voice dominating those of the health officers farther down, although it had been years since he'd seen either Room 127 or any health officer; he could hear the thud of colliding bodies (he could hear them rocking on their heels) coming from inside Room 223; he could hear the doctor's voice and understand the words coming from inside Room 221; he could hear the guard returning coming from inside Room 219; he could hear the voices of people in the woods coming from inside Room 217; he thought he could hear the whine of a bullet coming from inside Room 215 (he could then hear sirens — he could hear more sirens approaching); he could hear the sounds of crickets, like broken filaments tinkling inside a burnt bulb (coming from inside Room 213); he could hear canaries singing — he could hear their footsteps — (he could hear the musical structure, the improvisation fit perfectly with the background) coming from inside Room 211; he could hear the guns on the African battlefields coming from inside Room 209; he could hear red ants and black ants locked in combat (he could hear them calling to one another) coming from inside Room 207; coming from inside Room 205 he could hear people talking in low voices (so low he could hear the noise, the calculating machines ticking away upstairs and the cameras and microphones recording); he could hear the thump of a jukebox (coming from inside Room 203); he thought about the red and black ants as he passed Room 201; he could hear all sorts of sounds around him, and he could hear nothing more. He could hear nothing, and he could hear it all in such a different way. He stepped out into the hall and walked down toward the elevators. The elevator was resting at that floor. In the morning, the elevator was clean and bare. It was always never not clean and empty anymore. The elevator made him dizzy. As the elevator descended, Room 227 was holding the outer door open and he could see that the interior scissors gate was partially open. The numbers above the elevator doors lit up in different shades of colours, and he was excited by the changing numbers as the elevator descended. He stepped out of the elevator into the main floor lobby. Directly in front of him was a life-size portrait of a lovely girl of about eighteen. Her fellow, assorted occupants: a blonde girl with a mohawk, done up in punk; four men with black suits and briefcases; a young man in corduroy pants and Beatle-length hair; and a pretty matron in a cocktail dress. Each of the twenty-seven rooms on the main floor of the hospital opened onto a wide porch through a door wide enough to admit a hospital bed. The light through the vestibule illuminated a high drift of snow in the hallway.

Snow drifted over the plaque imbedded in brass on the marble floor in the hospital lobby. He stepped out into the moonlight softly toward an old window. He stepped out into the moonlight. He stepped out into the reflection of light off of cosmic dust. Had he stepped out into the open, he would have stepped out into the air. Had it been the morning, he would have stepped out into the morning sun. Had it been another hour at another time of year, he would have stepped out into straps of heat. Had he stepped out at all, he would have stepped out into the night, into the wind. Had it been raining, he would have stepped out into the downpour from the clouds. He would have stepped out into the rain. Had he stepped out into the soft white night, the snow would have crashed cars under his footfalls. Had it been a little later in the season, he would have stepped out into the snow — but perhaps it would have really only been slush by then. Dirty yellow sunshine between his toes. Had he been downtown, had it been spring, it would have been a downtown mist. Had the tension left him, he would have stepped out into the yard, into the yard or out into the courtyard to urinate. Only then would he have noticed the fallen leaves and realized that autumn had come. That the snow in the hallway, the snow over the plaque, was leaves wearing the reflection of light off of cosmic dust. Then he might have stepped out into the garden and faced the enemies: He would have stepped out into the garden; he would have stepped out into the dust of the driveway, the staring light of the driveway. He would have stepped out into the darkness and scanned the street; he would have stepped out into the street; he would have stepped out into the street as if he meant to cross; he would have stepped out into the street, ignoring the guardsmen who pressed close on all sides, but stopped at the sight of a small figure standing near the gate (had there been guardsmen pressing close on all sides, had there been a small figure standing near the gate). He would have stepped out into the deserted little street; had he needed them, he would have stepped out into the road and focused his glasses; he might have stepped out into the aisle of a hurtling, gently swaying car; he might have stepped out into the street, and two men might have brushed past him; he might have stepped out into the street, which might have been pitch, and bumped into a sailor in whites coming his way. He might have reached a sunlit meadow; he then might have very quickly stepped out into the clearing and watched. Had he stepped out, there might have been water that he might have stepped into, and he might have raised his voice and maybe shrieked loudly.

•

The cinder-block walls are painted in pastel colours and glossy white, enlivened by bright murals depicting fantasy landscapes. In the Annex, no murals relieve its institutional drabness; instead, one wall sports a bare sheetrock patch where a previous resident punched a hole. The unit's two Isolation Rooms[1] open off the Annex's dayroom. Each isolation chamber measures about eight feet square. A vinyl-covered mattress and a blanket lie on the floor; otherwise the room is bare save for the convex mirror positioned so that every corner of the room is visible from a narrow window in its door.

---

[1] Among other mechanical fixtures, two lights hung from the ceiling, rotating on a motor. One was a metal halide light that provided the blue light; the other, a sodium light, supplied the pink light.

The Watchman

•

1. The duties of the Watchman will commence at half past seven o'clock p.m., at which time he will visit the office to receive instructions for the night.

2. He is expected, while on duty, to be faithful and vigilant, to visit every part of the male department, and the outer walls of the female department, at least every hour during the night, making as little noise as possible, never conversing in a loud tone, and opening and shutting the doors as quietly as possible.

3. He is expected to be kind, gentle, and soothing in his manners to the patients and to use every means in his power to tranquilize those who are excited and to allay the fears and apprehensions of the timid; he will pay particular attention to the sick, the suicidal,

and those recently admitted, will see that the patients are properly supplied with water, when it is asked for, and will attend to all other reasonable wants; he will notice any unusual noise in the patients' rooms, endeavour to ascertain the cause, and, if necessary, report the same to the Attendant; he will notice anything unusual occurring during the night and enter the same on a slate provided for the purpose, and he shall report any irregularities, neglect of duty, or violation of rules that may come under his notice.

4. It will be the duty of the Watchman to look after the heating apparatus during the night; he must be very watchful against fire and, in case of its occurrence, must report it immediately to the Superintendent and officers without giving general alarm; he shall keep the hose and fire ladders always in good order and in readiness for use; he shall ring the bell at the hour for rising in the morning, and he will be expected to perform such other duties as may be required of him. At six o'clock a.m., he will be relieved by the Porter, and his services will not be demanded again till the time for duty in the evening.

Bellocq leaves the second floor

•

He entered the stairwell in the centre of the building and climbed to the next floor.

He put his foot on the first step and started up.
He was not able to gain his balance on the second step, and his body began to sway and fall backward. (Let us see what he achieves on the third step.)
"I stopped on the third step, my hand on the wooden rail."
He found himself starting the fourth step, and his mind would project into the future.
On the fifth step, there were rather few people, but they were of such glory and dignity that they seemed to surpass the others in power.
"When I stand on the sixth step, my phallus becomes

erect, pushing out my short linen skirt."

On the seventh step was the elephant that is named Airavata and the horse named Vchi-irckvam, the unicorn rishis, two-headed rudras, and four-legged monkeys.

"Now I'm on the eighth step."

On the ninth step, the soul burned gently.

On the tenth step were mice and rats (house and field).

On the eleventh step, he made prophecies about the future and (said) prayers.

There were windows on the first landing of the stairs:

"I spotted a strand of wire leading from the sill of the next window to the ground. It was tied to a bar just outside the window."

"I stumbled on the twelfth step."

"I put my foot on the thirteenth step and grasped the handrail. I started to pull myself up to stand on the thirteenth step, and the world shifted."

He was then perched on the fourteenth step.

"I was on the fifteenth step of the flight of twenty-two steps when the thing happened. The light was dim because one of the bulbs wasn't working and the only illumination came from a red light at the head of the stairway."

"I'm on the sixteenth step." He paused then, to catch his breath and look around.

It was an old, bleached broom handle, bone white, glimmering on the seventeenth step up, pushed safely into the angle of the stair.

A brass plaque was installed on the eighteenth step. (With your head supported by a burlap bag, focus on the nineteenth step up.)

(See yourself on the twentieth step, beginning to walk back up the staircase.)

He stopped on the twenty-first step.

He picked up a pebble on the twenty-first step and tossed it onto the twenty-second step.

On the next landing there was a door.

Part Two

Bellocq, Little Bellocq

Bellocq returns to his childhood home ~ Little Bellocq, fabulist

•

Bellocq's building is made up of a group of four units, each surrounding a spacious central court. This court is entered through a direct, unobstructed passage from the street. From the central court there are recessed stairways in each corner extending all the way to the roof, and with private entrances directly into each apartment.

The primary purpose of these open stairs is to do away with all interior passages and hallways and to provide each family with its own entrance from outside the building. The open stairs are in reality open on one side only, which gives not only a view of the interior of one stairwell but also a view of the well in the opposite corner of the court as seen from outside.

Every particle of material in the stairway is fireproof, and hardly a crack or a crevice is left in which dust or dirt may collect. The railings are of iron, and midway between the floors are iron seats to serve as resting places. To keep out rain and snow, there are hoods over these seats, projecting outward at the proper angle to accomplish their main purpose without excluding air or light. Smooth glazed white tile on the walls of the well and large panes of thick glass in the hoods are designed to catch and reflect every available ray of light.

Little Bellocq stands, staring through the railings down onto the courtyard. Two swallows, leaving a nest in the opposite corner, roll their bodies and fly away in the opposite direction of the sun: It is long before midnight on the fifteenth day of March, and a crowd had gathered at the Clear Water Temple. Some of the people had come from Nara, others from Edo. "Look! Bakuya Daikyu!" cried the people from Nara as they pointed him out. Then, from the other side of the courtyard, another swordsman walked out. A swordsman with only one eye. "It is Jūbei!" cheered the people of Edo. The two swordsmen stopped in front of each other. Daikyu bowed slightly and announced, "I am Bakuya Daikyu of Shinkage-ryū." Jūbei returned the courtesy and said, "I am Yagyū Jūbei Mitsuyoshi of Yagyū Shinkage-ryū." He then drew his sword and held it in a reversed grip. His right hand was pressed against the hand guard, and his left palm was against the pommel. He then raised the sword slowly in front of his body, blade upward and pointing away from him. This was the famous Tenchi Musoken (Heaven-Earth Dream Sword) posture of Yagyū Shinkage-ryū.

The courtyard dappled with sunlight. Looming in one corner of the courtyard is a steel sculpture by Alexander Calder called *Black Beast.* Snow laden, the beast glowers across the frozen stillness. On a summer afternoon, he is a gentle animal to clambering children. The leaves from the dogwood tree in the courtyard seem to weep from the heat. But it will weep with leaves, and with bare branches, and with white blossoms, and with red berries and birds in the fall. The courtyard dogwood (Little Bellocq is now at street level and glimpsing through the legs of the *Black Beast*) now carries buds and bright leaves.

Autoportrait: Mom

•

She had found the most wonderful doll and she had lost all her babyish dependence and pliability, but she had found her nose and eyes. She had lost the fifty cents with which her mother had entrusted her to buy a sack full of badly needed groceries, but she had found a marble — it clanked loudly as it rolled across the hardwood floors. She had lost her dog, the best friend she ever had, but she had found the dog roaming near her home, along with the skull of a rabbit, fecal stains. She had lost her new bicycle, but she had found a circle. She had lost her cat, a friend, but she had found a slimy crawling thing on the far side of a piece of fruit. She had lost her eyeglasses, she had lost them twice already, lost eight, but she had found them lying in a drawer. She had lost her way one evening, but she had found her true hunting ground at last. She had lost her top, but she had found her niche, work she believed in and could do well. She had lost her virginity, but she had found an early calling, the secret of sharing. She had lost it again, but she had found a Catholic priest, found herself drawn into it, watching him as he shook and twisted, then froze with the utter force of his release. She had found it really exciting when she saw him naked, found that he had the leather sausage, found it in the bag of this gentleman who was her lover, found there a more acceptable formulation of male–female relations than among her high-school peer group. She had lost it some way or other, but she had found the great coloured waves, the creative vibrations, the sound from above her. She had lost it in a park at West End at about nine o'clock, but she had found her body could not be seen against the background of the blossoms, that she was a pretty good actress. She had lost her hair ribbon in the scramble among the branches, but she had found a teething ring under a lily pad, a cardinal flower growing out of a small spot of sand in the rocks of the riverbed. She had lost a bobby pin in the jam, but she had found a spider that could write her father's initials. She had lost the smile from her mouth, but she had found the bits and pieces. She had lost all contact with her natal family, but she had found herself a projectionist boyfriend. She had lost her parents, but she had found herself not caring for them, or about what happened to them. She had lost her parents and gone to Kansas, where her brother had settled on a farm near Topeka, but she had found the house odd from the beginning. She had lost contact years before, had become a heroin addict, but she had found a mild amateur interest in photography. She had lost her sense of direction and was among unfamiliar streets, but she had found somewhere else to sit. She had lost the keys to two boxes, but she had found an Easter egg. She had lost control during the birth of her child, but she had found out how many children had died during sudden emergencies and on which nursing shift the deaths had occurred. She had lost all hope of her son ever getting better, but she had found the Sonata no. 3 in F. She had lost the infant son to pneumonia, but she had found his bed undisturbed when she went to the room next morning. She had lost a child, a sense of herself, but she had found herself shaking all over. She had lost her youthfulness, lost her youth, but her dancing evoked cheers from thousands. She had lost nothing of her superbly svelte yet roundly voluptuous figure, but she had found none. She had lost something, the romantic illusions of youth, but she had found a complete array of cosmetics. She had lost one job due to transportation problems and another due to downsizing, she had lost her health insurance, she had lost three hundred dollars at cards, but she had found what was left of a dark green, almost black, silk scarf. She had lost all romantic feelings for her husband, but she had found his money better than none. She had lost this man to madness, but she had found Frenchmen lacking in masculine aggressiveness. She had lost track of herself in the marriage, lost her temper and tried to kill him, but she had found a weapon in a drawer in their apartment. She had lost him after what she grimly recalls as "three years of total insanity over dope," lost her husband, had lost him, and most likely right to the very end of mortal life, but she had found a pornographic photograph among his possessions, threatening notes. She had lost a great deal of security, for one thing, because all the family income came from her husband's work, but she had found her husband's sickle out under the hazel trees on the slope. She had lost confidence in herself and how she related to men, but she had found what books she could on sculpture. She had lost her appeal, but she had found one last thing in the back of the drawer: an old white cotton bra with gunshell cups. She had lost her shoes, but she had found a fan and gloves. She had lost her ability to distinguish various perfume odours, but she had found how to communicate with plants and animals. She had lost her talent to write, but she had found herself talking. She had lost her furniture and all her clothes, but she had found so many things — once had seen a shower of dolls' wigs falling to Earth. She had lost her wits, her wits, and then her breath started coming and going, but she had found a rhythm. She had lost her psychic powers, but she had found them merely restricting. She had lost count of the years, but she had found all the traps sprung. She had "lost her grip," but she had found it and why she was holding it so tightly that it was cutting into the skin of her palm. She had found a way, through the language of figure and metaphor, to protect herself. She had lost all her worldly possessions, her treasures, but she had found toys in a box one day, two veils in a parcel. She had lost her command of the sea, but she had found a massive woman looking for her. She had lost her voice, had lost her voice and so lost her identity, but she had found it more in need of sweeping than many rooms. She had lost everything, everything and all, but she had found enjoyment in planning her own memorial service. She had lost nothing and learned nothing, but she had found life. She had lost 1.5 stone (9.525 kilograms) in weight over the last year. She had lost 16 pounds but said, "I'm feeling wonderful." She had lost 7 pounds, a satisfying bonus. She had lost one boot, but she had lost 10 pounds and learned more than half a dozen new skills, but she had lost 32 pounds. She had lost over 40 pounds since it began (33 pounds in six months). She had lost a coin and a button through a hole in her sack, found the button but no money, but she had lost 20 pounds. She had lost most of her hair, some of her eyesight. She had lost a five-sen nickel coin, a thumb on one hand a few years before, her hat. She had lost all the old interests, lost interest in sex, had lost it. She had lost her grandmother's brooch, but she had lost 15 pounds. She had lost the ability to write her name, distinguish right from left, put her glasses on, locate doors, and walk without bumping into things, but she had lost weight and her jaw was firmly set, but she had lost vision in her right eye. She had lost all her hair, developed foot drop and wrist drop, but she had lost several toes on one foot. She had lost three. She had lost about 30 pounds and she had lost a filling in a tooth, but she had so many teeth. She had lost an eye, but she had lost a further 7 pounds, making her weight 60 percent of the average expected weight for a woman of her age and height. She had lost a leg, the right one, but she had lost interest in food and had lost a lot of weight, a significant amount of weight, so much weight, but she had lost count. She had lost much sleep the night she had lost her pill dispenser, her prescription. She had lost three-fourths of her blood. She had lost three-fourths of her blood ("as much as she could"), her body temperature had fallen to 80 degrees. She had lost too much blood. She had lost so much blood. She had lost. She had lost the way to limbo. She had lost. Or she had won.

Little Bellocq goes on a picnic

•

When he was five, he decided that he wanted to go on a picnic. So his parents took him to O'Fallon Park, solemnly unwrapped a single sandwich and handed it to him. Bellocq fondled it and went home with a feeling that he had known glamour.

The mysterious corpse has a magic all its own.

—Neil Gaiman, *Sandman*

Little Bellocq reads a newspaper

•

Front cover

Blank page

Whose body was found in a dumpster by a scavenger; she also was a prostitute, well-known and well-liked by her coworkers. She died March 4
The photo shows a greenish tinge on a tree
The wound on her hand in the shape of a fox head
The bruise on her forehead the colour of greasy wool
Her body covered in paint, grease, chalk, ropes, plastic
The photo opposite of an epileptic with a missing tongue tip

Who was murdered and sexually mutilated, January 20
The photo shows the dead body and a barn swallow (*Hirundo rustica*) in a reservoir for liquid manure in a pig herd
The wound on her thigh in the shape of a huge butterfly with outspread wings
The bruise on her cheek the colour of water
Her body was made into an object to be displayed and looked at
The photo opposite of an owl with a missing claw

Who was stabbed to death and her body left in a man's rented room
The photo shows a left-hand vertical wedge and part of a middle vertical wedge
The wound on her foot in the shape of a *T*
The bruise on her arm the colour of limonite
Her body sporting high heels, long black hair, with polka dots covering her bare flesh
The photo opposite of a child with a missing ear

Who was sexually assaulted and dismembered with a chainsaw and buried in a shallow grave in a wooded area
The photo shows the expression on her face
The wound on her wrist in the shape of a parallelogram
The bruise on her shoulder the colour of maize
The lower portion of her body was absent, and the legs not simply drawn back
The photo opposite of a scene from a movie with a missing centre

Who was found in a ditch
The photo shows a woman in uniform, sitting in a van; in her right hand is a gun; with her left hand, she holds a cigarette to her mouth to inhale; she has a band around her forehead and a ponytail
The wound on her forehead in the shape of a fish
The bruise on her wrist the colour of a frog
Her body wearing a FAGGOT T-shirt
The photo opposite it an 8x10 of my mother on a horse, posing with a shotgun

Whose body was found on a trail near Wreck Beach
The photo shows an icy riverbank and a distant, barren landscape that could never actually be "touched" in "real life"
The wound on her right foot in the shape of a carpenter's vise
The bruise on her jaw the colour of curds
With her black-lace-corseted front to the camera, hers is the only face we see, but her expression is so stock, so standard
The photo opposite of a duffel coat with a missing toggle

Who was beaten to death and found in a downtown street, August 6
The photo shows an extremely minor segment of the building, the perfect relationship of all parts of the segment
The wound on her forehead in the shape of a two-headed dog
The bruise on her scalp the colour of the sea

With her lipstick and carefully plucked eyebrows
The photo opposite of a series of different shades of a colour with a missing shade in the series

Who was found in a dishwasher, dumped south of Chilliwack, BC, by a prison guard patrolling near the perimeter of a minimum security prison; she was identified through fingerprints
The photo shows her with her family in their front room
The wound on her leg in the shape of a hemisphere
The bruise on her temple the colour of surrounding objects
Her body was much younger than her face
The photo opposite of a man wearing a coat with a missing arm

Who was found by a train crew in the bush; she went missing July 31; she was found strangled to death and left lying beside a railway track
The photo shows logs being loaded from tractor arch to railroad cars (but the same method is often used in loading trucks)
The wound on her fingers in the shape of a V
The bruise on her "private parts" the colour of egg yolk
Her body was lazily distributed in a balanced sprawl as though he had tossed it behind him
The photo opposite of monster women with tentacles or snakes for breasts, evil, wild-haired women with missing arms or legs

Who was found March 25, smothered to death in her basement suite
The photo shows the object and its energy field
The wound on her head in the shape of a hydrograph
The bruise on her ankle the colour of brown eyes
The human body in fetal position
The photo opposite of a hydrocephalic child with a missing splenium

Who was stabbed twenty-one times in the throat and five times in the torso with two separate knives in June; however, no weapon was ever found; her skull had been fractured by one or more blows
The photo shows a view of the Steel Yards, with mixed-use commercial buildings fronting onto 30th Street and parking and additional residential uses tucked behind
The wound on her right side in the shape of a carbide jewel ice-skate sharpener
The bruise on her leg the colour of pale moss
Her body out there extended through infinite wires and radio waves that criss-cross the planet continuously
The photo opposite of a dress with a missing button

Who was reported missing from her blood-spattered apartment, June 10; the shower curtains, towels, pillowcases and bedding including bedspread, and curtains were all missing; the mattress on her bed was bloodstained
The photo shows a series of sculptures ("Monk — Doctor — Dealer")
The wound on her face in the shape of a (partially

deleted) rectangle and turned into a kinetic set of spirals and counterspirals

The bruise on her neck the colour of leaves

Her body was like a magnet, an invisible coil binding her flesh together

The photo opposite of a door with a missing panel

Who was discovered in a pool of blood in a Gastown hotel

The photo shows nearly three-dozen men and one lone woman posing on the hotel steps, palm fronds drooping from above

The wound on her thumb in the shape of a mahogany table

The bruise on her hip the colour of a sky

The key to her rented room was mysteriously mailed to the hotel

The photo opposite of an unmatched easy chair with a missing leg replaced by a paperback novel

Who was strangled and buried under leaves less than four blocks from where she was last seen; she went missing and within a half hour of being unaccounted for was being looked for; however, police would not look until the next day, when they found her body with help from a police dog

The wound on her leg in the shape of a three-cornered piece of orange peel

The bruise on her jaw the colour of a cat's fur

Her body was so buff that "even her breasts seemed to be flexing their muscles"

The photo opposite of a toy frog with a missing eye

Who was beaten to death and dumped naked in a parking lot, November 30
The photo shows her against a plain stucco wall, caught in a ray of light
The wound on her knee in the shape of a Buddha
The bruise on her face the colour of red poster paints
The body was positioned like she was trying to step off the elevator and it looked as if the elevator dropped
The photo opposite of a section of ladder with a missing rung

Who was a practical nurse, stabbed to death, November 9
The photo shows a pterional approach in the plastic skull with retraction of the soft plastic brain, opening the sylvian fissure
The wound on her breast in the shape of a walrus
The bruise on her hip the colour of your hair
Her body was placed on the public highway, where it remained several hours
The photo opposite of a car with a missing tail light

Who had been missing since August 6; she was a prostitute in the Main and Hastings area, which is where several others were scooped by a killer, and it is thought she may be another in a series of murdered prostitutes whose bodies have been found in the Agassiz area
The wound on her forehead in the shape of a reverse J
The bruise on her right cheek the colour of the officer's uniform

Her body was very much like my mother's body is now; there was a little bit of extra weight on the thighs and, you know, rear end
The photo opposite of a shirt with a missing button

Who was beaten, along with her best friend, Misty, then raped and drowned
The photo shows a crack that propagated from the surface
The wound on her forehead in the shape of a feathered wreath
The bruise on her forehead the colour of the wood itself
Her body was only one surface with only one side
The photo opposite of a man with a missing eye, his socket excavated like an apple

Whose dismembered body was found at Cypress Bowl
The photo shows a left foot with six toes
The wound on her arm in the shape of a mussel shell
The bruise on her chin the colour of the asphalt roof
Her body was preparing itself for childbirth
The photo opposite of a doll with a missing arm on a ripped sofa

Who was working as a prostitute and was picked up by a man wearing a pink and green ski jacket; she was found at 4 a.m. November 21 in a room at the Colony Motor Inn, strangled
The wound on her arm in the shape of a little girl
The bruise on her clavicle the colour of my T-shirt, my underwear

Her body was covered with light and dark spots like the guinea fowl
The photo opposite of a pair of feet, one missing a shoe

Who was found dead November 12 in an auto wrecking yard on Cordova Street
The extreme right of the photo shows a front end twisted into a nest of crumpled metal
The photo shows a young Filipina in her early to mid-twenties, dressed in khaki, with a rifle hanging at her back, barrel facing downward
The wound on her knee in the shape of a headless horse
The bruise on her chest the colour of the light source
Her body was a feast for the eyes
The photo opposite of a missing person's poster

Who was a homemaker and part-time cab driver, strangled and found in a parking lot, February 9
The photo shows her lover lolling in yellow swimming shorts and bikini top at the edge of the pool
The wound on her leg in the shape of a shamrock
The bruise on her toe the colour of urine
Her body was "well-developed" for her age
The photo opposite of Hotel Lafayette with a missing *e* in its hotel marquee

Who was strangled to death, January 12; she was a prostitute
The photo shows her standing hunched forward, eyes closed, because of the powerful winds beating against her

The wound on her temple in the shape of a round arch
The bruise on her temple the colour of her own shoe
Her tiny body swathed in a glowing white silk kimono
The photos opposite of two bodies, the one in the sea off Plettenberg Bay with a missing forearm and the one in the desert with the same forearm missing

Who was found dead, July 8, in her apartment on Main Street.
The photo shows an old man who is already a great-grandfather, sitting with his back facing a group of his grandchildren, who are staring expectantly in his direction
The wound on her neck in the shape of a spire tapering upward
The bruise on her back the colour of chameleons
Her body was lying on the living room floor next to a rotary-dial phone
The photo opposite of a square with a missing or cut piece in the region of the top left-hand side

Who was strangled in her home on December 2
The photograph shows the bride and groom sitting together
The wound on her head in the shape of a lotus
The bruise on her upper lip the colour of logs
Her body was being made whole again
The photo opposite of a mummified body with a missing neck

Who was beaten and strangled and found naked in

the lane behind West 24th
The photo shows the chief of police and a patrol car
in front of the town hall/police department building
The wound on her back in the shape of a cube (its
length and breadth and height are equal)
The bruise on her head over her right eye the colour
of toast
Her body was an implicit and explicit part of the ex-
perience of fieldwork and the collection of data
The photo opposite of a naked doll with a missing
plastic eye

Who was severely beaten and stabbed to death in her
apartment, where her body was found
The photograph shows cheeses stacked among and
on rodent pellets
The wound on her thigh in the shape of a box
The bruise on her thigh the colour of a bride's gown
Her body was not resistance or even a passive offer-
ing
The photo opposite of a plastic car with a missing
wheel

Who was beaten, sexually assaulted, and strangled
before being dumped in a lane behind Knight Road
The photograph shows three men bending to look
down an open manhole, and the caption reads: The
Other Room
The wound on her head in the shape of a griffin
The bruise on her eye the colour of bricks
Her body had been rhythmic motion, with new
movements emerging out of the regular movements
The photo opposite of a London puzzle with a miss-

ing corner and an extra wrong piece

Who was found beaten to death and sexually assaulted in Templeton Park on July 28
The photo shows a small brown woman lying on the
mud, coiled like a prawn
The wound on her right palm in the shape of a phallus
The bruise on her forearm the colour of your lips
Her body was still groaning
The photo opposite of a doll with a missing head and
a plastic toy radish with lots of crooked roots that
look like hair

Who was stabbed numerous times in her apartment
The photo shows the convicted assailant stomping a
helpless German shepherd mix, who is lying on his
side and crying out for help, yet the assailant's
mother is quoted as saying that her convicted son
"never beat that dog"
The wound on her thigh in the shape of a boletus
The bruise on her wrist the colour of the walls
Her body was found lying on a wooden floor, covered with a flannel petticoat and a chemise
The photo opposite of an airplane with a missing
window

Who was strangled with a tie, and her body was
dumped near 65A Avenue and 136 Street
The photo shows her in a ski mask and wool cap
tending to customers
The wound on her head in the shape of a bent knee
The bruise on her left hip the colour of purple

Her body was smeared with dog feces
The photo opposite of flying cranes carrying a massive box with a missing bottom panel

Who was beaten and strangled in a wooded area at
the bottom of the Chief
The photo shows that it was taken from an airplane
The wound on her throat in the shape of a spherical
wave
The bruise on her jaw the colour of my hair
Her body was kneaded and twisted
The photo opposite of a dog with a missing ear sit-
ting on a fire escape

Whose body was found in a rain-filled ditch
The photo shows a coffee plantation on a hillside
with small patches of rainforest in the background
and a "live fence" running up the left-hand side of
the hill
The wound on her left arm near her wrist in the
shape of a cylinder
The bruise on her neck the colour of tea
Her body was well-adapted to her harsh life
The photo opposite of a pair of glasses with a missing lens

Whose partly nude body was dumped in the bush
near Wiggins Avenue
The photograph shows not only how what is pho-
tographed, but also how a photograph in general appears
The wound on her knee in the shape of a square
The bruise on her cheek the colour of horses

Her body was arranged in a restful pose
The photo opposite of a young boy who was setting
up a chair with a missing leg in front of his parents'
house

Who was found dead, July 22, in Vernon Creek one
day after she went missing
The photograph shows a gradual diminishing and
fading away from the immediate foreground toward
the distant mountain
The wound on her leg in the shape of a rocket
The bruise on her right arm the colour of blood
Her body was in a state of "non-reaction"
The photo opposite of a hexagonal lattice with a
missing point in the middle of each hexagon

Who was found dead at the Abbott Villa Inn,
September 26
The photograph shows us what we would have seen
had we been there at the time
The wound on her chest in the shape of a youthful
head wearing a fillet and wreath
The bruise on her collarbone the colour of the parts
under the epidermis
Her body was dragged downstairs to a small room
in the basement
The photo opposite of someone with a missing
breast

Who was found slain beside a gravel road
The photo shows a vast field of profoundly green
cultivated rows
The wound on her thigh in the shape of a deep bowl

The bruise on her shoulder the colour of fresh meat
Her body was twisted, her head straining back at a
broken angle from her neck
The photo opposite of a beat-up Model T coupe with
a missing front fender

Whose badly decomposed body was found dumped
in bushes in a Saanich regional park, September 9
The photograph shows everything in sharp delin-
eation from edge to edge, while our vision, because
our eyes are foveate, is sharp only at its "centre"
The wound on her stomach in the shape of a pear
The bruise on her back the colour of petals
Her body was a "grandiose female matrix" from
which masculine aggression issued forth
The photo opposite of a dark fellow with a missing
front tooth

Whose remains were found near the Seymour River
The photograph shows neither people nor that sun-
like half-sphere, with its hidden crack
The wound on her knee in the shape of a shining
bean
The bruise on her lip the colour of a conch
A naked woman with very erotic breasts and a ter-
rific ass
The photo opposite of a triangle with a missing side

Whose nude body was found dumped behind a
house at 10th and Carolina, June 4
Q: The photograph shows some model automobiles
on what appears to be the model of a street, is that
correct? A: Yes

The wound on her left side in the shape of a toad
The bruise on her hip the colour of dental hard tissues
Her body was penetrated by sound and the mantras of gods
The photo opposite of a cracker with a missing corner

Whose skull was found in Stanley Park near Beaver Lake, July 17
The photo shows a water pump with the belt removed
The wound on her neck in the shape of a kind of rectangular truncated pyramid
The bruise on her head the colour of a star
Her body was quite swollen as if she had within it the fully developed Son of God
The photo opposite of a Morse code buzzer with a missing line

Whose body was found stabbed to death in a Mount Pleasant apartment
The photograph shows everything that can be seen by the naked eye
The wound on her throat in the shape of a spark plug
The bruise on her knee the colour of grass
Her body was slowly transforming into that of a snake
The photo opposite of a Plymouth Grand Voyager minivan with a missing hubcap

Who was found beaten to death at a Maple Ridge construction site, May 31
The photograph shows objects in sharp focus in and

across every plane, from the nearest to the farthest
The wound on her head in the shape of a clothespin
Her body was hard and muscular from fifteen years
in the kitchen and over the washtubs
The photo opposite of a chair with a missing back

Whose body was later found in a shallow grave on
the University Endowment Lands, April 7
The photo shows supply ships on- or just offshore,
with a supply convoy moving up the beach
The wound on her side in the shape of a rather irreg-
ular rectangle
The bruise on her left eye the colour of a mountain
Her body was made more beautiful in form and
pleasant to the touch
The photo opposite of a foot with a missing toe

Who was found beaten to death January 26 on the
second floor of a Downtown Eastside housing co-op
The photograph shows two men embracing under a
statue of Saint Hedwig, who seems to be giving her
sacrally superelevated approval — representative of
others as symbolic backdrop — as she stands on her
pedestal in the background, a mild and friendly expression on her face
The wound on her foot in the shape of a catenary
The bruise on her lips the colour of a person of
colour
Her body was as limp as her skin dress
The photo opposite of a cat with a missing paw

Whose body was found in the bush 13 kilometres off
the Lougheed Highway

The photo shows a female skeleton
The wound on her buttock in the shape of a lizard
The bruise on her hip the colour of the throat chakra
Her body was always manifesting itself, manifesting
a thousand bodies
The photo opposite of a sitting man with a missing
left face, left shoulder, and left parts of the chair

The photo shows a juvenile monkey using an adult's
back to climb down from some rocks; the photo opposite of a coat with a missing collar

The photograph shows older, worn-out, typical
"overworked, 'unfeminine'" females; the photo opposite of a quiet boy with a missing piece of chromo-
some

The photograph shows only the backlit clouds; the
photo opposite of chipped white porcelain cups, one
with a missing handle

The photograph shows a luminous outer surface
area of the Earth's sky from an altitude of 65 miles;
the photo opposite of a tricycle with a missing pedal

The photograph shows a definite pattern of points;
the photo opposite of a man's hand with a missing
index finger

The photograph shows us what is not really here; the
photo opposite of a moment from a missing word
contest

The photo shows a primate reaching one hand through steel bars; the photo opposite of Dad trying to hold me astride a plump, piebald pony of some 10 hands

The photograph shows half a dozen skulls scattered like white helmets across the forest floor; the photo opposite of a house with a missing front porch

The photograph shows a bull being followed by a disturbing crowd; the photo opposite of a fly with a missing leg

The photograph shows dead rats which the fumigant killed while they were eating peanuts; the photo opposite of a tiled walkway with a missing tile

The photograph shows a clear concentric pattern of a decreasing intensity of damage with increasing distance from the source; the photo opposite of a piano with a missing key

The photograph shows the condition of the body and the location of a wound; the photo opposite of a gun with a missing barrel

The photograph shows a monk in flames; the photo opposite of a leaf with a missing tip

Empty page

Empty page

Empty page

Empty page

Empty page

Blank page

Back cover

8 y/o   My brother likes rabbits, but I hate them,   and I
like squirrels,   but he hates them. I'll make up a
bad story about him   -- I hate him! Rabbits are very trouble-
some;   they smell a lot.   Well,
a rabbit is lying in bed   and papa rabbit says,
"I've heard that hunters are on the trail."   The
baby says, "Well, I have a smart idea.   Since those hunters
like to hunt,   we'll give them something to hunt."   And
the father says,   "What?"
And the baby says,   "Fetch me a lot of pillows."   And
they draw a lot of rabbits,   and they look real,   and in each
rabbit   is a piece of dynamite; so when the hunters
come,   they shoot at the rabbit, and those hunters
flew into China and said.   "I'm never going rabbit hunting again."
9 y/o   Well, this lion is troubled by mice. He's
sitting there   and doesn't know what to do   about the
mice.   He's tried everything,
so he calls the exterminator,   and the exterminator says,
"The only thing to do   is to blow the mice out,"
but the lion says,   "I've tried that and lost three houses."
"Why not make traps?"   "But the mice have certain things
that disconnect the traps and they always get the cheese."
'Why not try poison, then?"   "But that's impossible
because the mice know it's poison   and they'll never
come out." Finally the lion decides   he will move to Florida,
but when he gets there, he sees now   ... he's being troubled
by worms   coming through the floor.   So finally
he says,
"I'll go back and live in the jungle where I belong."
12 y/o   This picture takes place in Texas about five
thousand years from now.   Civilization is extinct,
An atom bomb has killed everyone,   and the
whole Earth is beginning again.
The remains of civilization   are the Spanish
arch   in the right lower corner.
On the top
are a few birds   looking for food.
There's a mountain on the left side,   and from a cave, a sort
of snake-bodied animal   is wiggling out.
He's going to strike the birds,   eat them,
and then go merrily on his way looking for more food.
14 y/o   An undertaker; he is very sad
because he is putting to rest   all these people.
He goes out one night and looks with remorse   at all the work he
has done.   He tries to find out how he can undo
his work.   He can do nothing about it.
16 y/o Mike Jensen is climbing the 1,000-foot rope that   leads,
though he does not know it,   to hell.
He pauses on his ascent   in the arena,
as he notices a woman sitting   in the second balcony,
feet wide apart.   Why is man always attracted
to frustrating glimpses   of women's thighs
and hairy organs,   when women happen to be a bit indecorous
in the way they sit? Needless frustrations,   must
train oneself not to be diverted   by such things;
the only worthwhile thing   is the whole salami.   So
upward he goes again,   but he slips when he
unexpectedly comes   to some thorns interwoven in the
rope.   And as he slips down the rope
at a terrific speed,   he is split in half;
as he lands in the sawdust of the arena,   he appears as two sides
of a cow,   newly delivered   to the
butcher   and waiting to be put   in
the icebox. But some people like warm meat;   and just as
spectators break   from the bleachers to uproot
the football goals,   many people with grotesque
apelike faces rush to rip at the red-purple meat.
17 y/o   The son with his sensuous upper lip drawn up, his feet
languidly held   apart,   and
his hand close   to his genitals seems to be-
in the midst   of a very pleasant dream.
The old man motions and chants,   believing
he has induced this dream   and
sleepy state. As the old man turns,
one sees that he has no facial features.
He wants the young man to awaken now   so he can suck some
of his youth from him,
vampirish   or something like that.   The
old man feels that then
perhaps   he will have a face again.   But when the
young man finally gets up,
he kicks the old man down and walks away.
18 y/o   The man is climbing up the rope. There is
a crowd chasing him.   He is viewing something.
Might be looking out to sea.   Looking for a boat
to come in. He'd be one of the men   to bring in the cargo.
He's alongside of the building   People are chasing
him   because he is on the side of a building.
He is in a hurry -- he is in a funny position.

People are mad at him   — he has no
clothes on.   Walking around the streets
naked. He is some character in history.   Brutus. He
wouldn't be looking for a boat after all   — just fleeing
from the crowd.
They are after him.   He took their money
— he wants to get rich all of a sudden   and retire.
He gets away.   — does not look worried.   Gets
on top of the building.   Gets on the road and gets
away.   He has no money with him.   So he gets
away somehow without the money.
19 y/o   The young woman stands nude on the
model stand.   But she is without detail,   no facial
features.   no teats, no fingernails.
The artist first paints small circles on her breasts   of
a very beautiful colour,   a wonderful colour,
like the colour in some shells he brought
from Acapulco.   But as he paints in more details,   she
becomes less, rather than more
lifelike and finally falls down
flat as if she were a mannequin.   The artist feels very tired
and sick in the stomach:
all this work for nothing.   He goes out into the
streets   and
sees
all his fellow mannequins mechanically moving about.
19 y/o   Liberatio has just flown from the womb which
hangs   lazily on the castle ramparts,
swinging in the breeze.   He dashes
over the bridge, pursued   by three
horrible mammoth turkeys,   with beaks lined
with alligator teeth.   The bridge expanse between
them   crumbles, dashing the turkeys against
the rocks below.   Temporarily safe, he looks back at the
womb,   and it now appears as a tremendous tongue
with four webbed feet.   But his safety is temporary,
for his supposed refuge ahead
is the city,
gleaming not from the sun   but from heavy phosphorus
powder,   which, having been put
layer on layer   on the outside of the building,
appears spongelike,   and when viewed closely
is not glamorous   but dusty and deadish.
The heroic view of the city from this distance is indeed deceptive.
19 y/o   Papa, your moustache, with its
horrid, dirty colour,   feels unpleasant on my cheek
when you kiss me. In fact, I feel uncomfortable   when you
come too near.   Why don't you embrace a bush?
It has the same texture.   And don't give me your old philoso-
pher's look.   Your philosophy is not objective
enough;   it's only based upon your own shortcomings and
frustrations,   which all hark back to the fact that you were
abnormally fond
to your mother.   And so Papa takes the
son's advice   and goes in the backyard to
a bush, but finds that it is his own father.
7 y/o   The father is getting washed to go
out for a big hunt   with his little boy.   They
will have fun.   The father is scrubbing and scrubbing   and scrubbing. He will get nice
and clean.   And they are going to stay out nice and
late.
and he doesn't want to get too dirty.
The little boy is getting his shoes on.
He will tighten them very, very tight.   They are getting their
clothes on and then they will go out
and hunt.   and when they get done,
they will eat.   Now the father is getting out of the bathtub
to get on his nice shiny clothes.   They are going to have a party
out there   for every kangaroo. They will have their food
— their deer and their wolf food.   and their tiger food.
They will have an awful lot of food.   The little boy is not
afraid   because his father is going to
be with him.   They have an awful long, long trip,
for they have good feet and do not get tired
a long while.   His father likes his little boy,   for
and the little boy likes his father   because the father
helps the little boy.   They are healthy.

Part yenta, part hustler, she claims that "much in the way flowers know their humble origin in dirt, women build their dreams here."

— **Lily Burana,** "Quality of Nightlife," *New York Magazine*

Bellocq's neighbourhood I

•

A few short years before Disney became the reigning commercial presence on the block of 42nd Street between 7th and 8th Avenues, the turf was ruled by the mother of all peep shows: the cavernous Peepland, which dominated the sooty promenade with its signature storefront of a giant eyeball peeking through a keyhole. But it closed down in the early nineties, and all that remains is the façade, long since patched over with plastic flowers and a giant mural of Dr. Seuss's Cat in the Hat, which smiles knowingly at the passersby below. Now a handful of little pod peep shows cluster in Peepland's wake, virtually identical to one another in their floor plans: books, videos, sex paraphernalia up front, palpable flesh in back or on a separate floor. If you prefer your pornographic diversions in live-action form, just follow the flashing neon that points the way to the LIVE! NUDE! GIRLS!

Bellocq's neighbourhood II

•

At dawn, as he steps out into the ruins of the courtyard, he is met by the cry of the muezzin proclaim-
ing that there is no god but Allah and Mohammed is
his prophet. In the courtyard are perhaps a dozen
young men, most dressed in white T-shirts. Some
disappear into a ground-floor apartment. Across the
courtyard at a window of a dimly lit room, a man in
undershirt and suspenders stands. In another window, a young girl who has washed her blonde hair
rests her head on the sill with her long tresses falling.
The courtyard is surrounded by a low white wall,
atop of which courses a long black grille, and this
grille is festooned with banners carrying utterly de-
fiant proclamations: THERE IS NO FREEDOM
WITHOUT SOLIDARITY! DECENT PAY INSTEAD

OF EMIGRATION! WE SUPPORT THE DEMANDS OF THE STEELWORKERS! All faced in, away from the world and into the harmless insularity of the courtyard. They were visible from outside the wall but only backward. The banners seemed to be shouting to each other in a vast prolonged but finally ineffectual tumult.

Bellocq and Grisélidis go to prom

•

This tableau is to be built in the town of _____,
_____. It will be an existing two- or three-bedroom
frame house with living room, kitchen, back porch,
etc. It will have to have a driveway, walks, etc. And
the yard will need perpetual care. All the windows
are to be painted black or mirrored so the interior of
the house is dark. The house will be furnished in for-
ties or fifties contemporary Sears and Roebuck
farmer style. It will be complete and obviously func-
tioning, with four people in the inhabiting family.
They have a dog and a four-door sedan which is
parked in the driveway. To withstand the weather, it
will probably be a shell of just the metal parts,
mounted on pipe standards or painted black or mirrored, etc.

In the driveway is a second car which has pulled up behind the family sedan. The driver's side door is open, and a dome light is on: It has obviously just arrived (again, concrete seats, tires, etc.).

Just inside the front door is a young man and his date (the girl from the family). They are standing close together, shyly intimate but not actually touching or embracing. She is in a prom gown (corsage). He is in a suit.

In one bedroom is the younger brother, sleeping soundly. In another bedroom is the mother, lying in bed stiff, listening (soft light illuminates the piece). In the kitchen, sitting at a table, under an unshaded light bulb, is the father, tired, rigid, menacing. He has been teased into letting his daughter go to the dance (this is her first real date). He doesn't know why, but right now he hates the young man.

•

The top of each stairwell is covered with a pergola. The pergolas have iron framework holding glass panels over the top and glass windows partway up the sides, with numerous sections which can be opened when desired. Immediately under its roof, the pergola is always open for ventilating purposes, but so that neither snow nor rain can find its way into the hall.

Little Bellocq stands, staring through the railings down onto the courtyard. Two swallows, leaving a nest in the opposite corner, roll their bodies and fly away in the opposite direction of the sun, away from the main courtyard of Divis Flats, a courtyard made from the incomplete foundations of basements. The unfinished basements in the main courtyard sit there like some postmodern Celtic ruins. The photographer had been shot at here the first time. He was at a party in the new row houses next door when he heard a commotion outside. He grabbed his cameras, made it through the ruins of the courtyard and underneath the concrete slabs that the cars park under, and almost bumped into a fifteen-year-old hood running from a soldier. The soldier stopped once inside the concrete alley, took aim, and fired. The bullet missed the photographer's head. A bonfire of scrap wood lit the courtyard, and around it stood two dozen little hoods. The same dirty cheeks, the same buzz cuts. "Hey, mister, give me fifty p." "Got a smoke, then?" "Take me picture." Fireworks tossed into the fire exploded, causing the photographer to turn suddenly, and the kids erupted in laughter. "You know Michael Jackson, mister?" "No. Hey, where are the kids with the cars?" "One came through 'bout half past — should be a lot tonight; it's Halloween." Just then a car came squealing down the street out of view, and everyone jumped to their feet. It squealed into the courtyard under the concrete slabs. Suddenly there were fifty kids all around it, the most ambitious already in the trunk of the car, while the most privileged exchanged words with the fourteen-year-old driver. Everyone wanted to know what he was going to do with the car when he was done with it. The driver teased them for a while, gunning the engine, flipping through the radio stations, toying with the high beams, until the trunk was unloaded and the car squealed out and back up the street. The whole exchange took about thirty seconds. The kids went back to watching their bonfire while the photographer left the courtyard.

On a wet summer day, the grounds around the courtyard take on the steamy aspect of a rainforest. The leaves of the dogwood tree in the courtyard seem almost to weep from the heat. This tree was particularly chosen for the private enclosed land-scape so that the families "can watch it with leaves, and with bare branches, and with red berries and birds in the fall." The stand of pines close to one of the ground-floor apartments provides heavy shade and, says one of the residents, "keeps us pleasantly cool while the rest of the world bakes."

Bellocq and Grisélidis have a dance

•

Fans vivisect the overcast sky and make the concrete rings of corrugated metal of the ceiling tremble. And then they die. The beer and soft-drink signs fade. Two skinny boys dance there, embrace, kick, like there is a thick-meshed fence between them, around them, which they lean upon like prisoners. A third boy, in a green vest with giant golden jewels on the back and white Thai writing, clings to the mesh netting cut into diamonds. Their heads shoot up and they lurch. One boy overpowers another, forcing his head down in a sport of rape or torture. But they smile as they nearly strike each other, with fisthammers, heelhammers. Cats wander about the floor. Nearby, old men (octogenarians, nonagenarians, centenarians) lay knees up on phony-granite

benches, breathing steadily, some with wrists in-
folded across their hearts so that their steel watch-
bands catch the cloudy light, others with their
fingers hanging over the edges of the benches. One,
by a gingko tree, with what looks like a faded astral
map tattooed across his front (thrashing lines, quarter circles, and captions of Chaldean incomprehen-
sibility). A young boy pours water into a big saucer,
laves it over him, encouraging and caressing him,
supporting his face and massaging his ribs. The boy
opens his pants and pulls something out, is trying to
massage energy back into his muscles. Lifting his
head, he sucks water from his ears. A slender man in
a T-shirt walks by. A smiling young waitress comes
around to take orders for soft drinks and to peddle
roses. Near her, Grisélidis and Bellocq are head to
head, dancing in their pain, holding on while mos-
quitoes bite silently. The sun is ending, in the frame
of the high hills and two church steeples. Bellocq
thrusts out his chin and raises his shoulder, flailing.
A young lady in red brings soft drinks to the spectators (open-mouthed, prancing, pushing each other's
shoulders, slamming their hips), and a white cat
comes out from between someone's legs. Grisélidis
whirls. Ankles flash high like swords. A foot grazes
a shoulder. Slender dancing knees and the sharp slap
of a foot against a rib. She gazes at her feet on the
dirty floor, breathes heavily through her open
mouth. She wears the face of someone enduring
pain: resolute, distorted, tightening upon itself with
a hissing. Bellocq grips Grisélidis in an expression-
less embrace that somehow involves the side of a
foot against a knee. Squeezed clinging and strug-

gling. Knee meets knee. Thigh meets stomach. Embracing at the neck, working their knees around each other's legs and buttocks. They lock knees around each other, some new and terrible way of making love, shouts swarming and ringing. Eyes like withered stems. Light-coloured garments hang in the darkness like moths. Cops in helmets and jackboots. To them, bodies and souls have never mattered. A group of young girls moves past wearing circlets around their heads with stiff rods in the back like the handles of frying pans. They stretch as they sway and flex, like dancing girls, caress and shake, arms upraised, mouths gaping. The air is hot with crowd sweat, eye-watering with cigarette smoke and the crying out of deep, ritualized shouts. Illuminated by their flashes of pain, shock, and triumph. The dull gaze of endurance. Sudden masks, perhaps just the strobelike effect of the fans cutting across the light tubes in the smoky humidity. Bobbing under a chain of beauty and violence. A pair whom no one cares about or bet on as they lean against the fences and grin at one another. They will fall together, flailing at one another with spread fingers, desperately striving to be birds, above the canal full of rising gray water caked with raindrops. Above the girls in yellow uniforms scurrying to the massage parlours. Above the drenched old man between stopped cars (eight abreast in the rain, and a motorcycle darting in between), selling newspapers in plastic bags.

•

All the exterior windows are extremely high, extending from floor to ceiling, and have sashes in three sections so that two-thirds of the window may be thrown open. Moreover, each apartment has a strong, spacious iron balcony reached through the windows. These balconies have no communication with each other and are sufficiently wide to be used as sleeping porches if desired. The arrangement of the rooms is such that no outside widows open on toilets or hallways. All of them are either in kitchens or bedrooms, and in a great majority of the apartments, there is a direct cross draught through the rooms, from the street side to the inner court, or from the courts separating the various units. Both the roofs and the cellars of the Vanderbilt buildings are in a sense the common property of all tenants. In the basements are laundries for the use of tenants who prefer not to do their washing in their own rooms, and the roofs provide ample space where children may play or for older folks to rest or do their light housework in the open air.

Little Bellocq stands, staring through the railings down onto the courtyard. Two swallows, leaving a nest in the opposite corner, roll their bodies and fly away in the opposite direction of the sun, while at 9:00, they close the doors, and Father Aristide begins the mass. Fifteen minutes later, the street in front of the church, Boulevard Dessalines, is suddenly filled with about a hundred Orphans, all wearing T-shirts and armbands. Shouting anti-communist slogans, they launch a storm of stones on the church. The first shots are fired as the congregation launches into a very loud hymn, in a show of courage and strength. It only takes the Orphans five minutes to force down the church doors and stream in, armed with knives, machetes, and pistols. Bodyguards move swiftly to protect Aristide as the congregation hides behind columns or under pews. The congregation is stuffed into the rows of pews, so the assailants' job is easy. They just walk through the church, shooting as they go. Two of them, lost in the excitement of the massacre, slice open the stomach of a pregnant woman with their machetes. Others tear apart the prayer book and scatter the sacrament. Currents of blood stream on the ground. Children, crazy with terror, run off in all directions. At the other end of the courtyard, the mayor directs the maneuver from his white car. The Orphans all worked for him. A group of them then douse everything with gas and set fire to the church and all the cars parked in the street. The wounded writhe in the courtyard.

On a late fall afternoon, sunlight floods the living room through the oaks and maple that keep it shaded all summer and in the early autumn provide a brilliant yellow and orange curtain. Light plays on a carefully chosen object. The courtyard dogwood (Little Bellocq is now at street level and glimpsing through the legs of the *Black Beast*) now carries buds and bright leaves.

Bellocq stares out the window

•

First, reflected in my window, I saw my own eyes. I saw my eyes and then watched my lips move. Looking straight ahead by the glimmer of my lamp, which stood in the window, I saw something further in human shape: a flash of movement, a very faint reflection of myself, features stepping forward aggressively, angrily (a funny-looking pinched-in suit and high-buttoned vest). Past this, in one window, I saw streaks of sunset. In another, only the glass and the wire netting. In another, a girl sitting down with a middle-aged man in a white coat, at a table playing cards. A thin hand waved a pork chop. I saw him bend her back, down on that bed in her room. In another, I saw coils of rope and blocks hanging from beams. In another, a woman sitting alone in her bleak and bare room with her pale face turned toward mine. Or perhaps it was an old skull or some strange-looking pot. In another, I saw a beard, a cigarette (like white eyeballs in a black man's face) and then was given the finger. In another, a man walked by in a canvas hunting coat, his lips moving. He looked at me as though he was scared and then his face disappeared. In another, I saw forms moving; it had lights; so I saw two shadows moving behind the curtains. In another, I saw a big blanket of a pattern I knew. In another, I saw two women walking down the hallway; they both wore conservative suits and carried leather purses big enough to conceal pistols. They both wore their hair collected in a tight chignon. In another, I saw a man with rimmed glasses completely naked, a young woman undressing, and then shadows on the blinds. A cat in the window; I saw it watching.

Like James Stewart

•

Like James Stewart, I was the photographer with a broken leg who sat at his back window, spying on his neighbours across the courtyard, what was happening in this life, my fear, echoed, amplified, and commented on by the events across the courtyard. The photographer who turns the film until number one appears in the first window. Then, after making an exposure, the photographer who turns the film until the same number appears in the second window. After the next "shot," the photographer who turns the key till number two appears in the first window, and so on. In one corner of the courtyard, a hummingbird rose and fell.

Bellocq's dad I: magnetic tape

•

Green was the colour of the room, and the carpet looked like it had been dyed with old bottles of India ink. There was so much unstrung, twisted magnetic tape over everything; the furniture appeared to be floating in the Sargasso Sea. Bellocq's dad lived looped in tape.

Bellocq's dad II: a tape recorder

•

We would be talking, when suddenly — without a word of preparation — Bellocq's dad would touch a button and his voice would emerge from a tape recorder. Then he'd get that look on his face that a ventriloquist wears when he's listening to his dummy, that unnaturally fixed, attentive yet abstracted look that masks the secret working of his voice.

Bellocq's dad III: a typewriter

•

Bellocq's dad was motivated by a touching love of print and the paraphernalia of learning. He was childishly delighted by Magic Markers, staple machines, clipboards, fresh Xerox copies. In the last months of his life, he learned to type, and this simple skill so delighted him that he could not be enticed away from the machine. His last words were a legal formula tapped out on a typewriter.

Bellocq's dad IV: a eulogy

•

When you split Dad into pieces, you knew exactly where to put them.

Dad dead is Dad docile. A dead Dad can be sorted, sifted, filtered, and distilled. You can pick out the good parts and throw the rest away. In the trade it's called "packaging."

Live, Dad was a problem. Dead, Dad is a property. Live, Dad was worse than obscene — he was boring, always ranting about dumb things like the First Amendment. I mean, really! Dead, Dad is this beautiful myth. He's got Esthetic Distance now, and the wild thing about E.D. is that once you've got it, the more whacked-out your behaviour, the better for the legend. People will dig anything, provided it's no threat to them. They thrill to the war on T.V. They can't read enough about the horrors of the ghetto. They never commit themselves to a hero until he's been assassinated. Well, mister, Dad qualifies.

The week before he died, Dad was so broke and so short of friends that he had to hustle his parole officer for ten bucks.

Death always loved Dad. But Dad was coy and wouldn't surrender. He clung to life with the tenacity of a dying comic.

Finally, he got so tired and sick he had to lie down. Death was gratified.

Dad is dead. Dad lives. Long live Dad dead! Repeat after me. So now let us celebrate Saint Dad and his miraculous Electric Resurrection. A bearded saint atop the pop pantheon.

I climb up on the cabin roof sometimes to let the stars into my eyes. But once I am up there they seem farther away than when I am on the ground. There is a constellation that reminds me of your hipbone. I think I am trying to get close to that bunch of light.

— Bill Callahan, *Letters to Emma Bowlcut*

Constellations

•

And that, that is part of Andromeda's hipbone. He touched her leg. She touched his hand.

And that piece is Antlia's piston rod. He touched her arm. She touched his face.

And that particle is Apus's brow plume. He touched her shoulder while the class was watching a video. She touched his hand.

And that bit is Aquarius's deltoid. He touched her blonde eyebrow. She touched his hand.

And that scrap is Aquila's scapula. He touched her lightly on the arm. She touched his arm.

And that bite is Ara's mensa. He touched her shabby coat. She touched his arm.

And that fragment is Aries's tail patch. He touched her hair and pushed it back from her eyes, where it had fallen again. She touched his cheek with her long, rough hand.

And that morsel is the top of Auriga's left foot. He touched her on the shoulder and arm. She touched his hand with hers when it was freed and sat up, a finger to her lips, while she rubbed her ankles to get the blood back in them.

And that crumb is the back of Boötes's head. He touched her arm, whispered encouragement. She touched his face.

And that speck is a tooth in Leo Minor's mouth. He touched her suggestively, talked filth. She touched his face gently.

And that speckle is the crook in Lepus's right leg. He touched her left breast. She touched his fingers. They were not cold. She touched his palm, felt the fleshy padding near his fingers.

And that stud is Libra's fulcrum. He touched her arm. She touched his feet and applied dust of his feet on her head.

And that shard is Caelum's bevel. He touched her butt and pinched her butt. She touched his arm and said, "Whenever."

And that notch is the end of Lupus's snout. He touched her lips. She touched his jeans and felt the material around his buttons strain and pull tight.

And that nick is the edge of Lynx's paw. He touched her throat, that throat that had been so savaged her voice was forever changed. She touched his trousers zipper.

And that cut is part of Lyra's frame. He touched her lips again. She touched his shoulder.

And that snip is Camelopardalis's long, long neck.

He touched her hands that had worked so hard. She touched his wrist.

And that snippet is Cancer's right cheliped. He touched her genitals through her clothes. She touched his forehead.

And that chip is part of one of Canes Venatici's two leashes. He touched her genitals under her clothes. She touched his shoulders.

And that stitch is Canis Major's snout. He touched her face and head with his hands. She touched his face.

And that splinter is Canis Minor's abdomen. He touched her face, then leaned her head back. Clumsily she touched his chest.

And that sliver is Capricornus's fluke. He touched her breasts again, both of them this time, not quite as lightly but still taking care to be gentle. Her nipples were taut with desire, and he wet them with the very tip of his tongue as he slowly trailed his hand down to her panties. She touched his shoulder and then his cheek.

And that shiver is the front of Carina's keel. He touched her, very lightly, just to see his long fingers on her. She touched his face.

And that smithereen is Cassiopeia's right knee. He touched her lips. "Strawberry and" — he skimmed down to the tuft of hair between her legs — "chocolate." When she touched his hair, her naked breasts touched his naked chest.

And that lump is Centaurus's two front hooves. He touched her breast. She touched his face.

And that gob is Cepheus's scepter. He touched her in between her legs. Dry. He moved her up higher on the bed so he could lie on his stomach and look into her. She touched his cheek.

And that hunk is Cetus's fluke. He touched her "cola," pointing to and touching her vaginal area. She touched his lips.

And that chunk is Chamaeleon's stereoscopic eye. He touched her (put your index finger at the bottom of the shorts of a stick figure someone has drawn). She touched his arm. She raised it up.

And that stump is Circinus's hinge. He touched her shoulder. Then she touched his belly.

And that flash is Columba's thumb feathers. He touched her jaw, his thumb caressing her lower lip. She touched his sleeve.

And that blaze is Coma Berenices's braids. He touched her thigh and jerked away as if her flesh were hot. She touched his swollen member.

And that flare is Corona Australis's browband. Again he touched her thigh, but this time he didn't pull away. She touched his forehead; it was very hot.

And that flame is Corona Borealis's ruby. He touched her arm. She touched his arm.

And that gleam is Corvus's black eye. He touched her mouth. She touched his erection lying hard against his stomach.

And that glint is the base of Crater's neck. He touched her hand in thanks. She touched his forehead lightly with her lips.

And that glitter is Crux's suppedaneum. He touched her face, then leaned her head back. She touched his chin affectionately and softly whispered some words as if she was in love for the first time.

And that glimmer is Cygnus's black bill. He touched

her cheek again. Then she touched his knee.

And that shimmer is Delphinus's median notch. He touched her hand. She touched his side. That curve there, under the arm.

And that twinkle is the tip of Dorado's bill. He touched her cheek. She touched his fingers.

And that blink is the middle of Draco's eye. He touched her "inside" the "lip." She touched his palm, felt the fleshy padding near his fingers. That skin had once been hard with callouses. Now it was soft and loose. She poked the middle of his palm with her forefinger.

And that sparkle is Equuleus's left nostril. He touched her vaginal area beneath her clothing. She touched his hair, she touched his face, she touched his throat, she touched his chest.

And that spark is a hinge along Eridanus. He touched her vaginal area. She touched his face.

And that coruscation sits in Fornax's combustion chamber. He touched her "private parts" with his finger, while he stood and she lay on the bed. She touched his brow.

And that spangle belongs in Gemini's hair. He touched her again, this time moving his fingers up and down along the line of her jaw until he touched her mouth. She touched his nipples and was surprised to find that they hardened and extended like her own.

And that flicker is a feather from Grus's primaries. He touched her jaw with the back of a callused index finger. Then she touched his chest, intrigued by the feel of his soft mat of hair.

And that flutter is the inner edge of Hercules's right

buttock. He touched her feet. She touched his hair.

And that quiver is Horologium's pendulum rod. He touched her skin. She touched his neck. She said something he could not hear, and when she spoke again, her lips were almost touching his cheek.

And that flickering is one of Hydra's scales. He touched her most private places. She touched his fingers. His nails were clipped short. She felt his wrists, traced the bones and veins in his arms.

And that fluttering is part of Hydrus's belly. He touched her fingers. She touched his cheeks. She touched his eyes. She touched his throat. She touched his head. She touched his forehead. She touched his lips.

And that sprinkle is the centre of Indus's spearhead. He touched her cheek. She touched his face. She touched his hand.

And that dot is the tip of Lacerta's tail. That was all — no, not all. He stared into her eyes as he touched her wrist. She touched his hair.

And that spot is a mat in Leo's mane. He touched her between her legs. She touched his cheeks, traced his jawline. "Smile," she said.

And that cleft is a foot of Mensa's leg. He touched her hand. She touched his shoulder.

And that gash is Microscopium's eyepiece lens. He touched her hidden bud. She touched his tongue with her own, lightly, and then again.

And that score is Monoceros's dock. He touched her crack with his finger. She touched his arm.

And that kerf is in Musca's right compound eye. He touched her neck and shoulders, then traced circles around her breasts and nipples. She felt them harden in stiff peaks as he moved a feather to her navel and abdomen. She touched his face, then she touched his lips.

And that jag is Norma's heel. He touched her with his lips again and felt her breasts with his hands. She touched his arm.

And that joggle is Octans's thumbscrew. His eyes lost their hardness, and he touched her nipples with almost childlike delight. She touched his hand, then his arm.

And that notching is Ophiuchus's right hamstring. He touched her breast, softly and then with a cruel twist. She touched his chest and let her fingers rest over his heart. She looked down and then touched his cock. He stepped back and then reached out to touch her ear, lips, and breasts as she had touched him.

And that serration is part of Orion's right teres major. He touched her hair. She touched his wrist, then his cheek.

And that sawtooth is the eye of one of Pavo's tail feathers. He touched her flesh, or pressed his lips against hers. She touched his cheek and then let her finger touch his lips.

And that denticulation is Pegasus's top lip, under the left nostril. He touched her peach-coloured cheek. She touched his shoulder, then she touched his other knee.

And that dogtooth is the right eye of Medusa, slain by Perseus. He touched her left shoulder. She touched his hair, the same hair she had played with just a few hours ago.

And that crenelation is Phoenix's lower mandible. He

touched her leg and the grass under it, and moved his hands up to touch her warm stomach and found her breast. She touched his mouth.

And that crenulation is part of Pictor's frame tray. He touched her cheek. She touched his teeth.

And that scallop is the top of Pisces's operculum. He touched her hand, running his fingertips lightly over the inner surface. She touched his chest, his stomach as it rippled quickly up and down.

And that rickrack sits above Piscis Austrinus's anal fin. He touched her "pee-pee," her arms disappeared into thin air. She touched his hair and his ear just as lightly.

And that deckle edge marks Puppis's roof. He touched her breast the way he had touched her hair, a finding in the dark, a mere grazing without demand. Then she touched his face like that again.

And that cockscomb is Pyxis's hinge. He touched her lips softly with his finger. She touched his feet with both her hands and then touched her forehead.

And that bristle is one of Reticulum's posts. He touched her again, parting her, running a long finger along her cleft, the pearl waiting there rising to meet him. She touched his neck.

And that barb is one of Sagitta's fletchings. He touched her breasts and vagina and licked her vagina. She touched his penis for "one or two seconds."

And that barbel is the smart waist joint of Sagittarius's bow. He touched her face with a soft caress and lifted her chin with a finger. She touched his jaw with her fingertips.

And that striga is Scorpion's first metasomal segment. He touched her face, caressed her cheek and her chin. It was a pretty chin. She touched his penis. *And* that seta is the handle of Sculptor's mallet. He touched her cheek with the tips of his fingers. She touched his penis.

And that stubble is Scutum's chief point. He touched her calf again with the point of a safety pin. She touched his side.

And that whisker is one of Serpens Caput's labial scales. He touched her shoulder, and her head lolled aside to enclose his hand. She touched his shoulder briefly.

And that scratch is one of Serpens Cauda's undertail scales. He touched her clitoris. She touched his face with the back of her fingers.

And that crack is part of Sextans's alidade. He touched her earlobe. She touched his lips and felt the brush of his breath.

And that chink is the tip of Taurus's horn. He touched her disheveled hair. She touched his foot ever so softly.

And that score is Telescopium's azimuth clamp. He touched her unvarnished lips. She touched his arm, for too long.

And that striation is one of Triangulum's bottom points. He touched her from the legs down to her feet. She touched his cock.

And that rut is Triangulum Australe's top point. He touched her still-damp hair. She touched his earlobe.

And that wrinkle is the edge of Tucana's bill. He touched her lower lip. Split. She touched his face with her fingertips, delicately running them over the planes of his cheekbones, down to the curve of his mouth.

And that chamfer is Ursa Major's trapezius. He touched her hair, then his fingers cupped the back of her head. She touched his tongue with hers.

And that pleat is Ursa Minor's brachialis. He touched her hair, which was caked with salt from swimming, the texture of straw. Stiff as feather quills. She touched his chest and shoulders and upper arms.

And that bezel is part of Vela's main head. He touched her breast, gently, admiringly. She touched his hand with pride.

And that crimp is where Virgo's shoulder begins. He touched her pulse. She touched his eye with a gentle fingertip.

And that rabbet is a piece of Volans's pectoral fin. He touched her breast on September 27, 1983. She touched his hair and watched him.

And that dado is Vulpecula's right stifle. He touched her vagina with his penis. At 9:31 he touched her, and they copulated from 9:32 to 9:42.

•

Their way around the tall cyclone fence across the street at the off-ramp. Stepping between the Wrong Way Do Not Enter and One Way signs, through the thick brush to a spot where the hobos had spread out some half-dozen mattresses. On one of the mattresses, a photograph of priests French-kissing trainee priests in front of the Christmas tree.

Part Three

The Minotaur

CASE No. 5374. — *J.F. Perseveration; some stereotypy; sound reactions; unclassified reactions, many of which are probably due to distraction. Note on test record states: "Understood what was expected but could not be induced to give much attention to the stimulus words; sat facing a window and showed a strong tendency to merely name objects in sight. Reaction time very short, in some cases so short that it is doubtful if he recognized the stimulus word at all."*

Table God, dark angel music, bird sickness, woman, man male, deep dove, soft dog eating horse, mountain mule, house dog, black rabbit, mutton, hen, comfort dog, hand clock, short (myself), fruit, post, butterfly bricks, smooth glass, command, sand, chair, leaf, sweet wood, whistle, earth, woman, grass, cold mustard, slow kale, wish, lampsquob, river, ten, white rock, beautiful water, window scene, rough, been, citizen, house, foot (stable), spider horse, needle, pin, red cushion, sleep (black), anger (white), carpet, vingency, girl, noodles, high macaroni, working tomatoes, sour asparagus, earth, oakry, trouble, peas, soldier, beans, cabbage greens, hard cow, eagle, robin, stomach, hawk, stem, fishes, lamp, whale, dream, shark, yellow crabs, bread, red, justice jam, boy (be), light girl, health, filth, bible, book, memory (bad), sheep, dat, bath (oval), cottage nurse, swift, begin, blue joy, hungry, wonder, priest, apostle, ocean preacher, head (dead), stove store, long, lone, religion, world, whiskey whisper, child, gule, bitter rugby, hammer, ball, thirsty sun, city Christ, square Jesus, Butter Joe, Doctor John, Loud Luke, Thief St. Matthew, lion, lie, joy George, bed Beth, heavy, tither, tobacco, iron, baby blade, moon, stars, scissors sun, quiet, wired, green mean, salt Lou, street vault, king, sepulchre, cheese, Presbyterian, blossom Baptist, afraid (Methodist)

●

There is a cornea; behind that is a lens. and behind
that a retina and nerve. and behind that a little skin,
which keeps the shell together. and behind that a
more remote space which the audience normally
cannot see. and behind that a patch of green. and
behind that a vague darkness of mountains which
run into dull-coloured clouds so that you cannot see
their tops. and behind that a remote but sharp and
vivid background. and behind that a yard, and in
this yard is a shed containing tanks and a copper, in
which tripe is prepared. and behind that a wall. and
behind that a crowded room with an open furnace
in the corner, in which silver is melting on red
glowing coals. and behind that a wall. and behind
that a very fine stable, like that commonly full of

Persian horses. and behind that a wall. and behind that a spruce plantation. and behind that a patch of woods. and behind that a row of houses and trees. and behind that a second, more irregular row of houses, an increasing number of which have iron roofs and walls of sawn planks. and behind that a sandbox. and behind that a lovely pavilion with a ceiling of woven rushes and of tapa cloth and shells. and behind that a tall green foliage plant in a pot. and behind that a swinging settee with a canopy, and on either side, toward the end of the platform, two settees, one of willow and one of mahogany. and behind that a bench for three. and behind that a huge, looming house. and behind that a range of twelve rooms. and behind that a door leading to the kitchen. and behind that a long narrow kitchen. and behind that a wall. and behind that a larder, twelve foot ten by fourteen foot six. and behind that a wall. and behind that a china room. and behind that a kind of sofa: before this was a little low form like what the priests have before them when we see them at divine service. and behind that a wooden wing. and behind that a Copenhagen snuff dispenser. and behind that a dope machine. and behind that a bronze of Apollo by Praxiteles. and behind that a big brown round-bellied pipe, the only ribald note in the room. and behind that a loose-hung drapery of embroidered stuff like the setting of a throne. and behind that a card reading: "Horehound Drops — Five Cents a Bag." and behind that a blue card. and behind that a wall. and, behind that, a toilet. and behind that a wall. and, behind that, a daybed. and behind that a gray record player. and behind that a wall. and behind that a bedroom. and behind that a wall. and, behind that, a green-tiled bathroom. and, behind that, a wall with windows, and, beyond that, shrubs. and behind that a separate building for the reception of lunatics. and behind that a greenhouse where turnips, kale, and kohlrabi are grown. and behind that a small garden for summer dining. and behind that a row of crocuses. and behind that a dark yew hedge. and behind that a cemetery with the strangest headstones. and behind that a pagoda shrine containing the usual bowl of sticks of incense and a mirror. and behind that a wood full of ghosts. and, behind that, a low-lying fog bank. and behind that a small flat triangular projection, like the spine of the ischium. and, behind that, a spark chamber. and behind that a little platform with a metal grille drain at the bottom. and behind that a Kershaw ballast regulator. and behind that a roller, and behind that a harrow. and behind that a ten-foot spike tooth harrow. and behind that a flat truck bed with curtained sides and a top. and behind that a Ford truck. and behind that a screen wall. and behind that a pasture with a brook in it, and butternut trees, and four cows — three red ones and a yellow one with sharp-tipped horns tipped with tin. and behind that a forest, where you may lounge through turfy avenues and light-checkered glades and quite forget that you are within half an hour of the boulevards. and, behind that, a long shallow bar, where, when the runs are in, the steelhead rest. and behind that a large boat filled with fused potassium chlorate. and behind that a rudder. and, behind that, a featureless brown land of stunted grayish trees. and behind that a road and railways. and behind that a barren landscape. and behind that a trench bunker system. and behind that a group that is just beginning to move in this direction. and behind that a hundred other faces pressing forward. and, behind that, a wall covered in slate. and, behind that, a light source. and behind that a brightly lighted backdrop. and, behind that, a ladder up which one climbs into darkness. and, behind that, a ruined warehouse. and behind that a narrow street of Chinese noodle restaurants. and, behind that, a bespectacled intellectual. and behind that a great power of digestion and assimilation. and, behind that, a light, a flame. and behind that a fire. and, behind that, a purpose. and behind that a legion of voices. and behind that a thousand years of Hellenic intrusion. and behind that a whole moral vision.

CASE No. 667. — *C.L. Pronounced stereotypy. Following note on test record: "Many attempts were made to secure a reaction other than 'cat,' but usually without success; the reaction cold — warm was given spontaneously and with apparent interest; most reactions were given only in response to much urging, or else mechanically, without attention."*

Table-cat, dark rat, music-shoe, sickness cat, man-boy, deep cat, soft hat, eating cat, mountain-hit, house-gold, black woman, mutton (get), comfort-cousin, hand-Jesus, short hat, fruit-hand, butterfly (going), smooth hat, command-boy, chair hat, sweet cat, whistle-boy, woman-cat, cold warm, slow button, wish (cat), river-cat, white rat, beautiful good, window-wheel, rough (good), citizen-candy, foot-cat, spider-dog, needle-cat, red button, sleep (cat), anger go, carpet-cat, girl in, high little, working cold, sour cat, earth-tag, trouble (cat), soldier-cat, cabbage-cat, hard cat, eagle-cat, stomach-cat, stem-hat, lamp-cat, dream-cat, yellow cat, bread-cat, justice-cat, boy-cat, light cat, health-cat, bible-cat, memory-cat, sheep-cat, bath-cat, cottage-cat, swift cat, blue cat, hungry cat, priest-cat, ocean-cat, head-cat, stove-cat, long cat, religion-cat, whiskey-cat, child-cat, bitter cat, hammer-cat, thirsty cat, city-cat, square cat, butter-cat, doctor-cat, loud cat, thief-cat, lion-cat, joy (cat), bed-cat, heavy cat, tobacco-cat, baby-cat, moon-cat, scissors-cat, quiet cat, green cat, salt-cat, street-cat, King Cat, cheese-cat, blossom-cat, afraid (cat)

The library

•

1. The Library of the male department shall be under the charge of the Supervisor. Every volume taken therefrom shall be charged to the borrower, except for the use of the patients, when it shall be charged to the Attendant, into whose ward it is taken, who will be responsible for its being used with ordinary care and returned in proper time.

2. If a volume shall be lost or destroyed, by any patient, the Attendant, having charge of the patient, will report the fact to the Supervisor and, if practicable, exhibit the fragments. If lost or destroyed by any other person, it must be replaced.

3. No one will be permitted to take from the library more than one volume at a time, or to keep a volume more than two weeks, without permission from the

Superintendent or Assistant Physician, except Bibles, Testaments, and prayer books placed in the hands of the patients for daily reading.

4. The Supervisor will be responsible for books taken from the library and not charged.

5. The Library of the female department will be under the charge of the Matron, who, in its management, will be governed by the above rules, prescribing the duties and responsibilities of the Supervisor.

CASE No. 3307. — *G.F. Unclassified reactions, mostly incoherent; slight tendency to respond by sound reactions.*

Desk (blue), stars, trees,
menace, soap, excited spelling

Marbles, train, bed, button,
steak (flexible), umbrella, blanket

Grass, sheet, carpet store,
flower, linen, water, coal

Ferry, sample, shades (blue),
suspender, wood, chisel, ruler

Snake, fly, bird (green),
opening (angry), stitching, madam

Ceiling (easy), warm heaven,
astonished man, carrot, softness

Parrot, mind, stable, oil,
awake, darkness, rough male

Buoy (standing) very ashamed,
staring stock, sponge, house

Mouse, fall, appetite, pastor,
waves, hat, blackening garden

Goodness, Kummell, woman coughing,
sofa, pillow (united, oblong)

Lard, physician, easy, burglar,
tiger (healthy), thread, gloves

Cigar, hood, stars, knife,
recollect: ring, pencil, bushes,
Germany, rice, pepper, allspice

...she delightedly bit into the astonishing stratifica-
tions that remained at her disposal, that is to say
sticks of chalk, and these wrote the word *love* on the
slate of her mouth. She thus ate a veritable little
chateau of chalk, built in a patient and insane style,
after which she threw a mouse-coloured mantle over
her shoulders, and with two mouse skins as shoes...

— André Breton, *Soluble Fish*

Bellocq writes some messages

•

He erased the word *buffalo* and wrote the word *supernatural*.
He erased the word *loafing* and wrote the word
arkade. He wrote the word a second time and a third
time. He wrote the word over and over until he had
written it one hundred times.
He erased the word *America* and wrote the word
slang. He wrote the word a second time and a third
time. He wrote the word over and over until he had
written it one hundred times.
He erased the word *artist* and wrote: "The word is
an illusion, said the Naturalists, it is an idol."
He erased the word *psychical* and wrote the word *perhaps*; he then crossed it out.
He erased the word *autonomous* and wrote the word

escritura on his pad, crossed it out, and wrote the word *oral*.

He erased the word *socialist* and wrote the word *painting* on the floor.

He erased the word *democratic* and wrote: "The Word is no longer guided in advance by the general intention of a socialized discourse."

He erased the word *open* and wrote: "closed forum."

He erased the word *China* and wrote: "USA." He erased the word and traced it with some chalk.

He erased the word *rob* (slave) and wrote the word *Calif.* following the word *State*, and wrote the letters *L.A.* following the word *City*.

He erased the word *Circuit* and wrote the word *groppo*. He wrote the word a second time and a third time. He wrote the word over and over until he had written it one hundred times.

He erased the word *LAW* and wrote the word in the lower case.

He erased the word *Revolutionary* and wrote the word for *whore*.

He erased the word *ἡμίθεος* and wrote the word *mountain* across the face of a woman in a magazine.

He erased the word *dismantle* and wrote the word *McDonald's*.

He erased the word *CRIPPLE* and wrote the word *emetli* (truth).

He erased the word *sister* and wrote the word *shadow*.

He erased the word *blank* and wrote the word *form*, then changed it to *shape*, and finally to *mien*.

He erased the word *Paradise* and wrote the word *omit*.

He erased the word *tum* and substituted *tantum*.

He erased the word *unconscious* and wrote the word *aphonia*, then erased it.

He erased the word *tomorrow* and wrote the word *saraballae*.

He erased the word *ibT31* and wrote the word *hypothesis*.

He erased a femperantian in red and wrote the word *curse*.

He erased a final *h*, and inserted an *s* between the stem-final *e*.

He erased the word *Muslim* and wrote the word *Palestine*.

He erased the word *colony* and wrote the word *humiliation*.

He erased the word *Jewish* and wrote the word phonetically.

He erased the word *soldiers* and wrote the word *young?*

He wrote the word *Bering* with the piece of blue chalk, wrote the word *probably*. He wrote the word *Industrial* following the word *Section*, and wrote the word *painter* following the word *occupation*, and the word *Painter's 644* following the word *Union*, and the word *yes* following the word *white*.

He wrote the word *triste* and wrote the word in charcoal.

He erased the word *ROAM*. In its place, his tongue protruding with the effort, he laboriously wrote: "ROEM."

CASE No. 1500. — *D.V. Considerable number of neologisms; stereotypy manifested partly in a tendency toward frequent repetition of certain reactions but mainly in a persistent tendency to make use of the grammatical form of present participle, giving rise to numerous doubtful reactions.*

Stand lonesome, playing disease,
hiding unreckless, beginning plenty
high standing, grivelling plenty,
laying disease, writing, coming,
flying, glomming, master standing

Sugar blowing loving cellar,
coming, dreaming, divided wall,
pleasant breaking, tumble gentleman,
sweating, biting, stinging coloring,
dreaming, widing, cleaning pretty

Degrace nobody, holling disgrace,
plenty shooting, welldebell earning,
setting degrivel, biting, burning,
walking, blowing, making unpossible,
growing stand, raising, teaching

Together weeding, held standing,
incuriossable, smooven, uncareless, going,
moving, setting, warm slowly,
everything burning, born taking,
hitting, drinking, welldebell taking

Soft instrument, speaking, gitting,
scared playing, laying raisen,
eating born, shining, cutting,
hitting landed, throwing, walking,
tension eating, growing nobody

•

He stepped out into the hallway. Families had put boards across their doors in anticipation of bulls charging down the hall. Curled up in the dim corner of a bench, a person-shaped shadow of a minotaur showed only its profile. He stepped out into the hall into what sounded somewhat like running horses, although it was alternately very strong and very faint. He presumed there were birds out in the hallway, pecking at the faded yellow-flowered wallpaper. He listened attentively. Yes. He stepped out into the hall, head down. He walked slowly with his head down. He stepped out into the hallway, cast a glance up and down its length. The pecking sounded somewhat like *ch*, sounded somewhat like *ts*, sounded somewhat like *ke-week, ke-week*. The hallway was running like a spiral staircase that runs up and up and up. He stepped out into the dimly lit corridor and, without looking back, closed the door behind him. He stepped out into the corridor. Frequently characters walked along the corridor in various groups, with the camera tracking along with them. Sometimes they came toward the camera, which moved more slowly than they, panned to follow them as they passed close to it, then tracked slowly after them. At other times the camera kept up with the characters, then paused with them as they stopped at compartment doors. He stepped out into the dark of the hallway in his socks, and the moisture in his socks turned into steam and sensitized his skin. He stepped out into the light, eyes focused straight ahead along the corridor, apparently unseeing. His overcoat was turned up and covered him to the ears. The light in the corridor had been switched on earlier. He stepped out into the passage. A naked bulb burned in the passageway. He stepped out into the passageway, ducking his head, although the lintel was quite high, but only moved a pace or two into the gloom before stopping and cocking his head back to listen. Above the lintel, there was a drawing dear to male adolescence: a skull and crossbones. He thought about the red and black ants a floor below as he made his way: a bird that sounded somewhat like a revolution coming from inside Room 301; the theme of a popular radio program that sounded somewhat like a bull coming from inside Room 303; a backfire of an automobile that sounded somewhat like a burst into laughter coming from inside Room 305; a cornet player that sounded somewhat like the bursting of a toy balloon coming from inside Room 307; an orchestra that sounded somewhat like the lisping of skipjacks coming from inside Room 309; rivers that sounded somewhat like the human voice when recovering from a cold coming from inside Room 311; the voice of some female canaries when they try to sing that sounded somewhat like crackers going off coming from inside Room 313; singing that sounded somewhat like a tin whistle emanating from a boiler foundry coming from inside Room 315; bullets coming through the switchy woods that sounded somewhat like squealing pigs and somewhat like hurt birds screaming coming from inside Room 317; knocks on a cardboard carton that sounded somewhat like machine-gun fire coming from inside Room 319; African-American preachers coming from inside Room 321 that sounded somewhat like Yiddish; wind through a barbwire fence that sounded somewhat like Chinese songs coming from inside Room 323; fans in the ceiling that sounded somewhat like a telemarketer reading from a script coming from inside Room 325. From beneath the door of Room 327, dirty yellow sunshine between his toes. With dirty yellow sunshine between his toes, he stepped into the stairwell. Calculating machines ticking away upstairs, and hidden cameras and microphones recording.

CASE No. 6164. — *L.E. Remarkably persistent tendency to give sound reactions; numerous sound neologisms; no reactions given in response to some of the stimulus words on the ground that she had "no word to match."*

Table witchhazel; dark frog; music lessons; sickness badness
man wife; deep seef; soft shoft; eating feeding
mountain sounding; house shmouse; black fake; mutton shutton;
comfort somfort; hand land; short court; fruit shrewd butterfly
shuddergy; smooth slude; command noman; chair sash; sweet leaf;
whistle noshissel; woman lemon; cold shoal slow snow; wish dish;
river liberty; white size beautiful   ; window Hilda; rough shoff;
citizen shiffizen foot shoot; spider shider; needle dreedle; red shred
sleep seef; anger   ; carpet shloppet; girl shirl
high fie; working shlirking; sour bower; earth world
trouble shuttle; soldier polster; cabbage sheffies; hard shward;
eagle   ; stomach   ; stem lamp; lamp sant
dream leam; yellow cherry; bread dread; justice chestnuts
boy   ; light shwife; health felt; Bible memory   ; sheep sheet;
bath scab; cottage foppach swift shift; blue shoe; hungry angry;
priest sheaf ocean notion; head shred; stove shove; long song religion switching; whiskey chiston; child kile; bitter shitter hammer
lemon; thirsty flrsten; city   ; square birds butter shudder; doctor
shoctor; loud souse; thief sheaf lion Zion; joy bloy; bed wading;
heavy shleavy
tobacco confecker; baby savey; moon shoon; scissors
quiet shiet; green sheel; salt shawlt; street freet
king sing; cheese seefs; blossom pleasant; afraid shraid

Bellocq leaves the second floor

•

He entered the stairwell in the centre of the building and climbed to the next floor.

And so everything then depended on the first step, everything depended on finding some way of taking this first step, of uttering the first word.
"Stopping on the first step, I had unaccountably felt a sense of pleasure, and so had proceeded to the second. On the second step, I had had the urge to compose a poem."
"In silence I regarded my shadow. There had seemed something strange and mysterious about the way in which it was arrested and broken by the edge of the third step."
(Let us see what he achieves on the third step.)

He sat down on the third step from the bottom and thought the problem over.

On the fourth step, he saw a vast number who looked like they were slain but nonetheless were alive. They were marked with brilliant wounds glowing like stars.

On the fifth step, to the right, a golden cat crouching in position; on the left, a chicken. On the right of the sixth step, a hawk was fashioned, and on the left side, a pigeon, and upon the top of the step a pigeon clutched a hawk in her talons.

"I was prevented from going upstairs by a tall figure in a black dress and wig standing on the seventh step."

"Now I'm on the seventh step. Now I'm on the eighth step."

On the ninth step, he told himself he could do something.

He caught his toe in a defective safety tread on the tenth step.

He ran out of fingers on the eleventh step.

On the first landing, he could see a chipped lavatory pan shining in the gloom of a windowless recess.

Something told him not to step on the twelfth step.

On the thirteenth step, there was a hard, rough, lumpy coating of ice about three inches thick.

On the fourteenth step, as he stumbled, he caught at the banisters.

"I paused to catch my breath on the fifteenth step."

On the sixteenth step, he went on all fours and loped as a pack of wolves does, grimacing and showing row after row of teeth.

As soon as he set foot on the seventeenth step, the statuette holding it became animated.

On the eighteenth step, he said, "I had feelings of God (*sentimenta Dei*)."

(Lie down on the tile floor and fix your eyes on the nineteenth step.)

(See yourself on the twentieth step, beginning to walk back up the staircase.)

The twenty-first step is even more wonderful.

A water mark was on the twenty-second step.

On the next landing there was a door.

CASE No. 5183. — *G.D. Neologisms; numerous unclassified reactions, mostly incoherent; some sound neologisms.*

Muss gone caffa monk
boy lesson ness pie
Gus muss court beef
ness koy ness dalb
flack mess cork ness
Bess toy girl cork
mass veil mouth cast
ness crow ratter zide
Malloy straw cast Roman
scack gois noise call
hort kaffir romerscotters bell
tramine gas cor kalbas
bell chenic trackstar loss
melso ormondo life quartz
nellan cor hallenbee book
bike armen cor callan
swar blacksen scatterbuck canon
men will somen lass
cor hanrow vand bike
hemmel cass cor malice
back ness arman cast
loss kaffir banrow cast
colrow boil padoc kantow
kilroe graft semen pess
guess tiffer cad mellows

●

The room is bare except for the imaginations of twenty children. Sometimes a room is totally bare. The room is bare to increase the acoustics. The end of the room that would be occupied by the players is practically bare, while that that would be occupied by the listeners is sound absorbent. The tiny area is empty except for a battered piano and some equally battered wooden folding chairs. The room has simulated iron bars all around, giving the appearance of a cage through which the occupants look out. The next room has been stripped absolutely bare. Is bare enough. Bare except where spots create circles of light. The floor patterned like a checkerboard. The floor is bare. A large beetle follows into the room in which half the windows are broken, the closet empty. Bare fluorescent lights over each window. Otherwise, the lighting is a combination of inexpensive bare-bulb fixtures mounted behind a fascia board around the perimeter and a dropped soffit into which three pin down lights are recessed. Old bare bulbs often transform a cellar into a bright, cheerful room. The next room is bare except for a bare-chested man. A bottle resting on his bare chest. Bare from the waist up, except for a red bandanna kerchief, soaked with cool water and knotted about his neck. Across the room, another bare-chested man grimaces as he lifts a leg. Again and again he lifts his leg, the effort and determination showing on his face. To the wall, a poster girl willow thin. The next room seems uncommitted, bare. The room is too bare, and you want it to appear smaller. The next room is bare except for an old travelling bag, which serves as closet and chest. The walls are bare, and you need some lamps. The next room seems bare and empty, with part of it given over to storage space. The next room seems suddenly bare, hollow of everything except a blue suit. The next room is totally bare save for the desk, the rug under it, an atlas stand, and an altar candle. A next bare room, with only computers and two chaises longues placed dead centre in head-to-toe position. The next room, loaded with ashtrays and open books (outside, the hum like assembly-line machinery) was otherwise bare, so you finish up by sweeping the floor. The room is now wholly unremarkable in every way. It had been a bathroom. All the fixtures have been removed, the window has been bricked up, and the room is utterly bare.

Remembering the room and himself in the room, a man, smiling a little, steps to the door lintel, twists the light switch in the wall, and removes it. He reaches into the hole and pulls out a rusty spike, bent at the sharp end. He turns, walks across the narrow room to the opposite wall, and begins to hack at the brown cement between the tiling. Something comes away and falls into his hand. A piece of brown bread, very dry and very hard. The room has a very low ceiling and is overlit; the effect is to crush in upon him, exaggerate all scrutiny. He has the old, wounded bitter-mule look of a nag whose teeth have been counted too often. You open another door and step into a cooling oven. There is a steamy, sauna-like heat, and the room is bathed in a garish orange radiance. The orange light emanates from a bare light bulb which is coated in a sticky orange substance, as is the window. The temperature of the room has recently been extremely high. The walls are radiating heat. Condensation is running down the window. Heat has cracked one of the windowpanes. The light bulb is bare because the plastic lampshade has melted, oozed down over the bulb, and fallen to the floor. The walls, ceiling, and all surfaces are coated with a greasy black soot. In one wall is an open grate, which contains the dead ashes of a coal fire. The hearth is tidy; there is no sign of any coals having fallen from the fire. On the floor, about one metre from the hearth, is a pile of ashes. On the perimeter of the ash, furthest from the hearth, is a partially burnt armchair. Emerging from the ash are a pair of human feet clothed in socks. The feet are attached to short lengths of lower leg, encased in trouser bottoms. The socks are undamaged. The room in which you find yourself next is bare, except for some loose lumber and rubbish, and the floor is rotten in places. There are two doors on the same side of the room and some windows in the opposite wall. In the next room, except for a collection of rather limp and drooping poinsettias from Christmases past, there is really no adornment of any kind. The walls are pretty bare. A bare, drafty hole with a mirror, flanked by two electric space heaters. A bare room with a cot, a candle, and a pitcher of water. Bare except for the bed and a rusty radiator that isn't putting out much heat. In the next room, tables are jammed on the floor, while the back of the room remains bare. All the walls are bare except for an unframed etching of Marx that rests on top of one bookcase. Next, a white-walled room is bare except for a bed with a gray blanket, a toilet without a cover, a shelf for clothes, a cement table, and a barred window. A spider-lashed eye painted inside the toilet bowl. A neon phallus on the room's ceiling. Well-shod feet holding up the table. You can still see the gray chinoiserie wallpaper between expanses of bare brick. The removal of layers of old paper to the bare walls yields a marvellous gift: original sketches of architectural detail done as working drawings by the first master carpenters. Sometimes these chambers have been little more than bare boxes. Sometimes they have been with elaborate devices for varying the quantity and quality of the air. Sometimes the subjects of the experiments have been obliged to breathe over and over again the same air. Sometimes the air has been kept under careful control and changed in various ways. The effects of the various conditions have been observed and recorded. Sometimes the room is bare.

CASE No. 4752. — *H.J. Neologisms; some unclassified reactions, mostly incoherent.*

Meadow black sweet dead
manion near sooner formble
gair temble benched ranched
bumble semble simber narrow
Ben gum bramble low
temper bensid hummery gunst
bemper tip gumper Andes
giinper hummer geep humper
zuper gumper himper gumper
moop rumble slamper Mnker
bumper gumpip imper gumper
humper guipper phar her
damnornott dumper gumper huntenit
hungnot bampir gumper sidnerber
eeper huntznit geeper himpier
hummer hunner bemnitper gumper
dumper dipper hummer rump
himmer hiniper gamper humble
gumper numper himmer gehimper
gueep humper deeper bummer
bimper harner harner himmer
humour gumpier homer doomer
per homer gumper gumper
humper gueet rummer numper
himper guinter yunger yunger

The Minotaur

•

and unwound a ball of thread and made his way
and unwound a ball of yarn and made his way
and unwound the hair from a ball of wax and made
his way
and unwound a ball of soft clay and made his way
and unwound a ball of metal clay and made his way
and unwound a ball of lead and made his way
and unwound a ball of twine and made his way
and crumbled a ball of cork and made his way
and whittled a ball of wood and made his way
and unwound a ball of linen rags and made his way
and unwound a ball of string with a peg attached
and made his way
and unwound a ball of green leaves and made his
way

and unwound a ball of leather and made his way
and unwound a ball of wool and made his way
and melted a ball of wax and made his way
and unwound a ball of white cotton wool and made
his way
and opened a ball of dense black smoke and made
his way
and undid a ball of plasma and made his way
and unwound a ball of earth and made his way
and unwound a ball of paper and made his way
and unwound a ball of clay on a spindle and made
his way
and unwound a ball of putty and made his way
and carried with him a ball of fibres from the epidermis of moriche leaves
and a ball of pitch to stuff in the Minotaur's mouth

the noise of the glazier repairing the window
the noise of the camera
the rolling noise of the tires
the noise of large diesel trucks
the noise of hand dryers in public toilets
the noise of the tape
the flicker noise of the audio amplifiers
the noise of a phonograph amplifier
the noise of atmospheric attenuation
the noise of a typical engine-driven electric genera-
tor
the phase noise of each of the free-running oscilla-
tors
the noise of the loop filter
the thermal noise of the feedback resistor
the noise of the electromagnetic field

the noise of her love
the noise of the weapon
the noise of this book
the noise of literature
the FM noise of an injection-locked oscillator
the loud noise of traffic on the busy street
the noise of battle
the noise of lamentation
the noise of media
the noise of a heated metal dipped into water
the phase noise of the probe laser pulse train
the detector noise of a low-light-level video camera
the noise of language
the noise of the great shout
the noise of beating
the noise of beating
the noise of hammering brass
the noise of history
the self-noise of microphones
the noise of fire being extinguished in the clouds
the "clack-clack" noise of the wings of the butterflies

and underwater noise of rain from the Minotaur's
mouth and magnetic noise from the Minotaur's
mouth and loaded asynchronous motors from the
Minotaur's mouth:
cerebral brushes, control-major counter banks, dials,
digit thrombosis with its aphasias, agnosias, and
electric accounting machine gang summary punch
apraxias
International Business frontal-lobe tumours with
joke-making, uncus tumours, machine jack plug lists
with hallucinations of chronic card fields, class selec-

tor connected alcoholism with its characteristic psy-
choses

lethargic encephalitis with its disturbance of minor
total print nnnnn nnnnn nnnnn the general con-
sciousness and its psychoneurotic o o o o o o sequel,
lesions to vascular hammerlock lesions with their
unilateral pathological feeling-tones

subtraction in the globus pallidus o o o o o-o o-o and
their motor consequences, pulmonary tuberculosis
o — o o — o o — o OOO OOO OOO with its eupho-
ria, and endocrinopathies like ooooooo o»o,
plugged print banks print myxoedema taste and
smell

infantile cerebropathies with their resulting imbecil-
ities, counter auto reset reset auto start auto syphilis
followed by general paresis, typhoid balance coun-
ters, card columns, card count fever and its toxic
delirium

exophthalmic goitre with their group indicator
punch gang summary punch pathological mental
states. Tantrums with imaginations

Acknowledgements

My thanks to Jon Paul Fiorentino, for all the places you continue to make for innovative writing in Canada.

A special thanks to George Elliott Clarke. I am particularly thrilled that you both read and cared about this unusual book.

Thank you also to Mike O'Connor and Dan Varrette at Insomniac Press for all of your editorial talents. This task was no small effort.

Work from *Leap-seconds* has appeared in the following magazines and anthologies: *Boulder-pavement*, *BLACK & BLUE: Revolution*, *The Calgary Renaissance*, *CV2*, and *Matrix*. My thanks to all of those involved.

My gratitude to those who have given and continue to give shape to me and my work: Gregory Betts, Weyman Chan, Kris Demeanor, Kit Dobson, kevin mcpherson eckhoff, Tyler Hayden, Dave Hibbeln, Jani Krulc, Marc Lynch, rob mclennan, Peter Midgley, Nikki Sheppy, and Natalie Simpson.

A nod to the talented writers with whom I shared the shortlist for the 2016 Robert Kroetsch Award for Innovative Poetry: Geoffrey Babbitt, Laurie Fuhr, Lea Graham, Ian Kinney, Micheline Maylor, and Diandre Prendimano.